For my very tolerant wife, Tammy.

This crime thriller features Joe Patterson, a dishevelled British private investigator and an unconventional hero who's trapped in a mundane life. Joe's life unravels as he takes on a case to locate a missing girl. He is forced to use his professional skills in new ways; to fake his own death, travel to sunny Malta and identify the kidnappers. The island is anything but paradise, as Joe discovers the influence of the mastermind behind the kidnapping and the true purpose of the criminal network under his command.

One

I'm sleep deprived and thirsty, in this humid hell. My hands are numb from the tight handcuffs clamped around my wrists. Sweat trickles from my hairline and beneath my t-shirt, down my back. These annoyances and the stress from the irate policeman in front of me muddle my thoughts.

"Talk, or rot in here," the Maltese officer yells in my ear.

"Okay, I'll talk," I gasp.

I screw up my eyes in disbelieve at the thought of being locked away in jail indefinitely. I stretch my fingers and clench them to get the blood circulating. I hear the slam of the solid metal door on the far side of the cell and open my eyes to see that my tormentor has finally left the cell. Thank god.

I sit alone on an uncomfortable metal chair in a twelve feet square brick box room inside a Maltese jail, in the middle of who knows where. The blindfold they forced over my eyes before the officer brought me here now hangs around my neck.

In an act of futility, I clumsily stumble to the door and lean awkwardly against the handle. Yep, of course it's locked.

I must be in an interview room, as there's a wooden table etched with scratches and ringed coffee cup stains. There's also a slightly more comfortable looking chair in the room, clearly for the interrogator. I sit again on my hard seat.

Above me, a single small vent pushes hot air towards my face. It must be over thirty degrees Centigrade in here, which is slightly above average for Malta in the middle of May. I would welcome a cool breeze, but there's no window to open. I'm completely contained.

There's a clunk and the door opens. A different officer steps in. He looks to be in his mid-thirties and I hope he's going to play the part of 'good cop'. He wears a long-sleeved light blue shirt, which is perfectly ironed and has what I presume to be the Maltese police emblem sewn onto the uniform at the top of each sleeve. He's also fashioning a thin black tie and navy blue trousers. After closing the door he takes the seat opposite and places a thick A4 folder and a police badge on the table.

"Hello, Joe. I'm Inspector Peter Bosco," he says in near perfect English. "Do you understand why you're here?"

"No," I say quickly.

"You've been brought in for questioning over offences relating to drug production, drug dealing and people smuggling. We've got enough evidence to put you away for *life*." he says sternly. "These are serious offences Joe."

"I'm innocent and happy to talk. But first, please can I get out of these cuffs? My hands are killing me," I ask and rattle my clasped hands against the back of the metal chair.

Inspector Bosco rises and takes a key from his trouser pocket. He walks round and clicks the cuffs open. I rub my red raw wrists as he sits again.

"We know you're at the centre of a drugs cartel," he presses, unmoved by my wincing.

"I've got nothing to do with those monsters."

"Thirty five years in a jail like this one, but with worse food. Is that what you want?" he asks. "I thought you were ready to talk?"

"I am."

"Well then, tell me everything you know about the drug network and those involved."

◊◊◊

It was a typical weekday morning in Crystal Palace, London. As usual, the piercing shrill of my alarm woke me at the unsocial time of six. I'd always wanted one of those clocks which glows warmly and wakes you with ever increasing natural light, but couldn't justify the expense on my meagre wage. I grunted as my feet touched the cold wooden floorboards.

I'd been wallowing in self-pity for almost a year after the death of my younger brother, Ron. I was going through the motions of living, but lacked the will to do anything. I missed him so much. There was no doubt about it; I was deeply depressed.

I guess Jennifer, my wife, had seen this in me long before I acknowledged it myself. At first she'd been supportive and caring after my loss. My parents were both dead, Ron had never married and he had been my only sibling, so it was just Jennifer and me representing the family at the funeral.

Ron's death was sudden. The coroner described it as a tragic accident, but every part of me knew it wasn't. The bloody driver racing through the streets that night didn't give a damn about anyone but himself. Ron was thrown through the air like a rag doll.

I tried to fight through those dark days of mourning, but was smothered by a blanket of depression that sucked all my energy. I piled on three stone onto my middle aged torso, as food was a source of comfort, but only a temporary drug, never lasting long.

I found work to be the best anaesthetic, as long as I was busy. So I worked late. I guess Jennifer just lost patience with me.

I pulled my work shirt around my bulging stomach and sat on the side of the bed listening to the springs of the mattress twang as I got my socks and trousers on, which made Jennifer stir slightly. Tip-toeing downstairs, I grabbed some toast before stepping out into the cold air. I clicked the front door closed behind me. Both Jennifer and Stu, my son, were still in bed as I stumbled down the dimly lit road to the train station.

I consider myself to be a morning person, but only after my first cup of coffee, and even then only when the Sun is above the horizon. I'd yet to experience either of those warming pleasures that morning, as it was winter and the cafe outside the station had a ridiculously long queue. I didn't bother waiting, but took a paper and left the exact change on the counter.

I sat on my usual seat on the train and turned on my iPod. I worked through The Times newspaper crossword. I enjoyed the daily challenge and battled through the clues for the next thirty minutes. I turned the pages to browse the rest of the paper. A full page holiday advert caught my eye, which pictured a distant exotic beach.

My mind drifted to imagine that promised paradise. I could almost feel the soft golden sand between my toes as they sank with each step towards the ocean. The waves were gently breaking on the beach, releasing foamy bubbles that crawled towards me. Overhead a single wispy cloud floats in an otherwise perfect blue canvas. The horizon is pleasantly exposed across the ocean but for a jagged rocky outcrop in the middle distance, which tempts me to swim out and explore it.

I heard distant music. It grew louder. I recognised it as The Beatles. I'd been asleep and slowly opened my eyes to see three fellow commuters sat opposite looking back at me. I was worried that I'd made a fool of myself. I touched around my mouth and apart from the unintentional 'designer' stubble I couldn't feel any dribble, thank goodness. I hoped that I'd leaned against the window in my unconscious state and not the poor woman to my right.

The rhythmical noise of the train as it rolled over the seams between the rails slowed. I glanced between the scratches on the window pane making up the message '*Linda 4ever*' and noticed that the train was stopping at the usual no man's land just outside the final stop, waiting for an allotted platform.

"This is the guard speaking. We're held by the signal outside London Bridge. We should be movin' soon. Don't forget to take all of your bags when leavin' the train. London Bridge is the final destination. All change please. All change," he said over the crackling speaker.

The man opposite me turned the page of his Financial Times and begun frantically highlighting share figures with a red pen. This stoked bad memories of a disastrous financial decision I'd made months before when I bought company stock that then slumped sharply. Jennifer went mental when I told her that I'd lost the money we had been saving for a new kitchen. I swore I would never 'invest' in stock again. It was sickening to see my hard earned cash slip away at the whim of the markets.

The train heaved forward with a jerk to the platform and stopped. The doors opened and people dissipated across the concrete. My claustrophobic feeling eased as I sat watching the young and eager push through the dispersing crowd. I reached into my pocket and selected Coldplay's latest album, which was something I had quickly become addicted to.

As I took a step into the aisle, my left shoe stuck to a fresh piece of tacky bright red gum. I wiped it on the floor, which removed most of it, before I continued to the train doors.

I walked the final half mile of my commute briskly. As I entered the office door the familiar Monday morning odour of stale curry accosted my nostrils. The leftovers from the company Friday lunch curry lingered over the weekend. Mr. Singh of 'Singh's Curries' next door gave us generous discounts, so Greg Webber, our company Director, had insisted on a weekly curry, with mixed results. He and I liked curry but there were some, like Alice, the company PA and video surveillance expert, who couldn't stomach spicy food.

The fact that Greg had never reached into his pocket to pay for these company takeaways reflected the financial success of 'Professional & Confidential Investigations Bureau Ltd'. Greg didn't pay well but I enjoyed the work and didn't have the knowledge or inclination to do anything else.

"Good morning," Alice beamed, as she sat pretty at the front desk, dressed elegantly in a designer blouse with her blonde hair held up with a wooden hair stick thing. It looked trendy, but I had no clue what it was called. She had a smile which stretched wider than it should, as if she had too many teeth in her mouth. There was more to Alice than met the eye though. She was a force of nature who had successfully kept in check the pack of often disorderly men who made up the company as well as being the company's surveillance expert.

"I've got gum stuck to my shoe and now I'm late. Not the best Monday morning," I said.

"Try putting your shoe in the freezer," she suggested seriously.

"Some other time, maybe," I said with a frown.

I walked down the narrow corridor and turned into the main office, where my desk was situated with six others, although two were just collecting dust because Greg had let two private investigators, or PIs, go. I'd been quietly confident that my position was safe though as I had a great case closure rate. In the PI business, success is measured in keeping your clients happy and closing cases. I also specialised in surveillance. We all had multiple roles in the firm, as we couldn't afford to turn away any work.

Trevor and Brian were both out at meetings. Ben sat at his desk, which was closest to the door and next to the row of three-drawer filing cabinets that contained the company records and live client files.

Ben was in his mid thirties, with the looks of a twenty year old. He used to be a professional bodybuilder and still took full advantage of his lunch breaks to visit the local gym. His muscles, or possibly the steroids he must have been taking, definitely affected his intellect; he certainly wasn't the sharpest tool in the box.

"It works. I've done it. The gum freezes rock hard and comes right off, without any hassle," Ben said loudly.

"Morning Ben," I said.

"I told you so," Alice called from the next room.

Like a trapdoor spider, Greg scuttled out from his office on the far side of the room, grabbed a book and disappeared again. He oozed urgency with a rack of lines across his forehead that screamed 'I'm busy and important.' He seemed to move, speak and think at twice the speed of any other human I knew.

"Aren't you going to ask me?" Ben suggested, while he held his finger behind his ear like an annoying schoolboy.

"How could I forget? How was the big date? Was she the woman of your dreams?" I asked half-heartedly.

"Not exactly. I took her to that Thai place you were on about in Covent Garden. Good food. By the second glass she was putty in me hands. By midnight we were rippin' each other's clothes off and she rode me like a cowgirl," Ben said.

"Too much information. Glad it went well."

Ben enjoyed a bit of banter, but he was a little crude for my liking. There was a part of me that was jealous of Ben's misadventures, but I would never admit it to him. I dragged myself away from his sordid escapade and headed to the mess that was my desk.

Thankfully, my success at the company had never been measured by the neatness of my desk. The message light was flashing on my phone and there was a Post It on my screen that read 'Come and see me. Greg'. I threw my bag down and headed to his office.

"Morning Greg."

"Joe, come in and close the door," Greg said, while he searched his desk drawers.

I sat opposite his oversized desk and looked up at a framed letter of thanks from the Metropolitan Police Service and a key to the city of Birmingham for his services. I had never asked Greg how he got that key. Next to it, pinned to a cork board, were several posters of missing people. Some were not even teenagers when they had just disappeared into thin air.

"I've got a new case that I need you on. It's for your eyes only. Could be very good for business," Greg said, with his head still buried in his desk drawers.

"Sure. Who's the client?" I asked.

"Read this," he said, as he pulled a file from the bottom of his drawer. "It should answer your questions. I want you to make this a priority. I've got to run now. Okay?" He passed me the file, stood up and grabbed his coat.

"Okay... Thanks,"

"Cool," he said and disappeared out of his office, leaving the door open.

I was left none the wiser as I stared at a blank vanilla coloured file, while also thinking that Greg was too old and senior to use a word like 'cool'. He was definitely not down with the kids and it just sounded wrong coming from him.

At that time it had been five years since Greg had started up his own company, after leaving a rival PI agency. He asked me and a couple of others to join him as he had transferred an impressive client list from the old company. Given Greg was only a couple of years older than me, I had been jealous at his ballsy and confident venture.

He had me persuaded quite quickly though, thanks to his gift of the gab and a possibly because of a touch of naivety on my part to believe every word he said. It had seemed like a golden opportunity which had to be embraced. It would have been stupid not to jump onboard. The possibilities, opportunities and long-term benefits were too inviting.

Things changed after just a few years. The hype and buzz faded as the clients diminished. I saw Greg lose his boundless confidence as the company struggled during the 2010 recession. Greg had been forced to downsize, but was quite cutthroat about it. He laid off two family men without a hint of remorse.

He became more detached from us, his workers, as he fought for more lucrative contracts with large insurance and technology companies and the like, sometimes abroad. He left us, his pawns, to mop up the small-fry of missing people and infidelity cases, while he pioneered work in larger fishing grounds. Job security was no longer a certainty. We all felt like we had to fight to prove our worth.

As I opened the paper file my phone rang next door, so I went to answer it.

"Morning, Joe Patterson here," I spoke into the receiver.

"Joe, it's Anne. Have you got anything new to tell me today?"

In August 2011, Anne Close had discovered a love letter in her husband's sock drawer. The heat of that summer had clearly driven Bill to have an affair despite, or maybe because of, twenty years of marriage. Anne had been a housewife out for revenge. She'd turned to a private investigator to get to grips with the facts of Bill's infidelity before taking him to the cleaners. I had sympathised with Anne. She certainly didn't seem to deserve to be cheated on, but she'd called me constantly, which was a real pain that I had to endure daily.

"Nothing new this morning Anne. Sorry," I said.

"Sorry, it's my fault. How can you be expected to find anything when I'm calling you all the time?"

"No, don't worry..." I said quickly.

"I just feel so awful and angry. I need to understand why he did this to me. I can't sleep or eat. My life is falling apart, but I need to know more before I confront him."

Conversations like that had been normal in my line of business. The work was not all secret cameras and tracking people. I'd learned over the years that it was equally important just to be there to listen to your clients.

"I'm sorry to hear that. I hope to get some answers for you very soon," I said.

Two

I found myself nursing a Diet Coke in a quiet bar on a Monday night. I wished it was a beer but I needed to stay alert. I'd learnt to like the taste of Diet Coke, after being diagnosed with diabetes a few years previously. Sugar was now a sworn enemy of mine. I was advised by my doctor to inject myself with an insulin pen before every meal. I didn't always take my illness as seriously as I should. I hated injections and the idea of injecting myself was horrible, so did my best just to keep my sugar input to a minimum. I figured it would be okay.

I had been sat in the bar for an hour and had twice told the nosy barman that I was waiting for a friend. He probably assumed my date had stood me up or I was simply a loner. Frankly I didn't care what he thought. It was important for me to get there early to scope out the exits and find a suitable place to sit. I liked to be familiar with my surroundings before a mark arrived, to limit any surprises.

A guy with a five o'clock shadow strolled through the bar and sat one seat away from me.

"Evening," he said.

"Hey," I replied while I looked down at my phone.

I had positioned myself in the far corner of the bar with a perfect view of both doors. Nineteen patrons had come and gone while I had been stuck to my seat, but none had been Anne's husband, Bill.

I was at the bar because I had got a lucky break earlier that afternoon. Bill had received a suggestive e-mail from his new squeeze, Dani, asking for them to meet later at this bar '*for some fun*'.

Anne had given me Bill's e-mail address and completed a detailed questionnaire about Bill, which provided me with all the information needed to crack the account password, after only a few hours effort. I then had access to all of his contacts and historical e-mails. Gold dust to a PI.

I had no idea what Dani looked like, but given that the bar was occupied by three couples, a mob of rowdy bankers at the darts board and Mr. Stubble, I was confident she had yet to turn up.

I carried a photograph of Bill in my jacket pocket in case I needed to remind myself of his appearance, but I had a good memory for faces. Besides, I considered it unprofessional to be staring at a photo of your mark as he walks through the door. It makes you feel instantly suspicious and your reflex is to cover the picture quickly, which in turn draws attention to yourself. I wouldn't make that rookie mistake. My mobile buzzed to life. Not ideal timing, but it could have been worse. It was Jennifer.

"Hey" I said quietly.

"Where are you? You were going to pick up Stuart from football," she said.

"Didn't you get my text? I'm seeing a friend tonight."

Seeing a friend was our code for me meeting a source. It was the perfect code as my job was all consuming and I had very few real friends anymore, as I had pushed them away. I text Jennifer instead of calling because I couldn't handle the angst whenever I changed her plans. I was just trying to get my job done but she never saw it like that. She always thought I was inconveniencing her.

"I guess I have to get him then?" Jennifer said impatiently.

Just then, I saw Bill in the corner of my eye appear from the darkness outside and push the bar door open. A gust of cold air pierced the warmth of the bar as the door opened and he walked in.

"Sorry. Gotta go," I whispered.

Bill patted Mr. Stubble on the back while saying something I could not make out and then sat down next to him. He raised his hand to get the attention of the barman. Out of professional curiosity, I wanted to know who Mr. Stubble was.

"Not yet. I need you to drop Stuart at school tomorrow," my wife said on the phone.

"Yep, okay. Really got to go now dear," I whispered and turned the phone off.

Jennifer was an events manager who on occasion was required to get in early to set up corporate conferences, seminars and the like. She didn't enjoy early starts and so often persuaded her colleagues to cover for her. She was a strong willed woman who was never shy about asserting herself. That was a quality that first attracted me to her.

That telephone call with Jennifer had resulted in me missing the crucial introduction between Bill and Mr. Stubble. The most likely time when two people use each others names during a conversation is when they first meet. I was annoyed. I sipped my Coke as I listened to their chatter, but still glanced at the door as I waited for Bill's bit on the side, Dani, to turn up.

"I haven't been there before. What sort of music do they play?" Mr. Stubble asked Bill.

"Just wait and see. You'll love it," Bill said in a camp voice, while he placed his hand on Mr. Stubble's.

Was that Dani? Was Dani a man? I thought to myself. I smirked as I foresaw the awkward conversation I would be having with Anne the following morning. Unfortunately Bill saw this momentary juvenile facial expression and stared squarely at me. It was stupid of me to have lost concentration like that.

"What's your problem?" Bill said aggressively.

"Nothing. I was just leaving," I said.

I downed the last third of my Coke and stood to leave. Bill also stood and with no warning leaned across and swung at me, connecting with my jaw. I stepped back in shock as my lower face split with pain. I supported myself against the wall and held my face in my hands.

"Screw you," Bill screamed as he stepped towards me. His yellow stained teeth sneered.

"He's not worth it babes," Dani intervened, holding Bill back by the arm.

The barman and other customers stared as I edged to the door, still holding my face, which stung like hell. Stepping into the darkness I realised the night couldn't have gone any worse after first insulting and then being hit by the mark. I'd been anything but professional. I just wanted to go home and forget all about it.

The next morning I woke to find the bag of peas that were pressed against my chin the night before had thawed and dampened the pillow and top of the bed sheet. My jaw had swollen and was painful as hell to move. Jennifer rolled over from her side of the bed.

"What happened to you last night?" she asked dopily.

"Had to work," I muttered, trying not to move any facial muscles.

"You don't normally get hit in the face at work," she said dryly with no hint of empathy. I got up in a huff and headed to bathroom.

"Remember, I'm leaving early today, so please drop Stuart at school," she called through the door. I turned the shower on and planted my head under the warm water.

Stu was my only son, I loved him more than anybody. He was seven going on forty; wise for his years, but sometimes a bit cocky for his own good. I got dressed and Stu greeted me as I aligned my tie in the bedroom mirror.

"Hey Dad," he said, "My jumper's got a hole in it."

"Morning Stu. Never mind. Get another one from your cupboard," I suggested.

After a final tweak, I was content my tie was straight and we headed into Stu's room, which had recently been upgraded from Thomas the Tank Engine land to a space port. There were posters of the planets and some spiral galaxies around his bunk bed. I dug around his wardrobe and found him another school jumper. He put it on and we went downstairs. Jennifer was in the kitchen finishing her coffee.

"There you are," she said to Stu. "I made you toast."

"Thanks Mum," he said.

Jennifer handed him a plate of hot buttery toast, cut into four pieces.

"Gotta run. Have a good day boys," she said and kissed him on the head. "Try not to get into any more fights today," she stared at me with an evil eye, before trotting out of the kitchen.

"Bye," I called, just before she slammed the front door.

I turned on the kitchen television to Bob The Builder and then got my own breakfast. "That's for babies," Stu said and got up to change the channel.

He sat back at the table and munched his toast in silence. There was a familiar morning rattle at the post-box. I poured a coffee and went to explore what the postman had left. Disappointingly, there was a credit card bill and a pizza pamphlet, along with an intriguing letter addressed to me, but with no further markings or indication of what was enclosed.

I opened it to find a thick application form and a cover letter, which read 'Mr. *Patterson, following your interest in a life insurance policy we are happy to enclose an application form...*'

That was an anti-climax. I'd been enticed by an advert two weeks before promising '*protection for the ones you love when they need it the most*' and so with Stu's future in mind, I text a free number for the paperwork. At the time I felt proud of myself for being so responsible. However there is a difference between asking for a free form and putting your money where your mouth is. I needed to read the small print. I folded the content of the envelope and tucked it into my work bag for some other time. I glanced at my watch. We were running late.

"Stu, time for school," I called from the hall.

"I don't want to go," he said.

"You have to go. Come on," I replied sternly, while tying my shoe laces.

A silence emanated from the kitchen.

"We really have to go, now."

I stepped back from the front door into the kitchen. Stu was sitting there, looking sheepish.

"I don't want to go to school today, Dad," he said.

"We all have to do things we don't like. Come on, please."

"No," Stu yelled and ran passed me and up the stairs.

Bloody hell. Kids. I instinctively and rather pointlessly glanced again at my watch, kicked my dirty shoes off and ran upstairs after him. I heard sobs of tears from Stu behind the bathroom door that he had locked. This was very unlike him. I wondered whether he had picked up on the tension between Jennifer and me. I'd read somewhere that children do sense arguments between parents however much you attempt to hide them.

"Stu, what's wrong?" I asked through the door.

"I'm scared. Don't make me go," he said.

"Open the door," I said and rattled the handle.

"No. You can't make me," he yelled.

"You can't run away from your problems, Stu. You need to face them," I said.

"You don't," he retorted quickly.

"Don't be cheeky, young man. Open this door *now*. I'm going to be late for work," I yelled through the door.

"Go *away*!"

I'm not proud of the thing I did next that morning. My blood boiled and Stu must have thought I'd turned into a monster. I kicked my right foot clean through the lower panel of the wooden bathroom door in an effort to swiftly open it. Stu screamed in fear of his own father. I regret it to this day, but at the time I really didn't give a shit.

"Argh!" I screamed in pain as my leg jammed between the splinters of the door.

Stu screamed and he started to hyperventilate. I was powerless to do anything. I felt foolish and stupid to have put myself in that state. I fell to the floor and eased my leg out. A large wooden shard cut through my trousers and was stuck into my calf. I felt queasy looking at it but was distracted by the view through the jagged hole in the door of Stu quietly sobbing on the floor. I took a deep breath and pulled the splinter out. It bled, but only a bit.

"Stu. I'm sorry," I said. "Please open the door."

He scampered out of sight to the other side of the bathroom. I didn't blame him. I put my arm through the hole in the door and reached up to the lock. Click. I pulled myself to my feet and opened the door to find a scared little boy curled up at the side of the toilet.

"Don't hurt me!" he screamed covering his head.

Three

I pulled myself together, bandaged my leg and wiped the stream of tears from Stu's cheeks, before we left the house. His little face was bright red from his distress. We pulled up to the gates of Cranley Primary School in my car. Out of guilt, I gave him a chocolate bar from the glovebox. He got out, dashed past the standalone school notice board covered with PTA notices, went through the main gate and crossed the empty playground.

I saw children's heads bobbing through the classroom windows. I knew Stu had missed registration and foresaw the phone call from his grumpy teacher reprimanding me about the need for good time management. He opened the front door and disappeared inside the school. I'm still not certain how I convinced him to go in that day, I think he may have simply been too scared of his own father. I engaged first gear, re-joined the traffic and sped off to the train station.

The train was less crowded than normal because rush hour had already past. The grey buildings and bridges passed my window as I read. Among the dreary articles about tax rises and cuts to public spending there was something far more terrifying; a full page article about an Indian school girl who had disappeared in London two days earlier.

A recently taken photograph at the centre of the page portrayed a pretty little girl with sparkling eyes and a lovely smile. A pang of horror stung me at the random nature of the loss of the infant. God knows what had happened to her. A smaller picture showed the mother and father clutching each other's hands at a press conference. I was so glad not to be them.

By the time I'd limped purposefully through the office door, the thoughts of the morning drama had been pushed to the back of my mind. Alice stared at me from her vantage point at reception, her eyebrows creased with concern while she conversed on the phone. Ben rose from his chair with his mouth gaping as I entered the main office.

"Your face looks messed up," he says, pointing at me.

"Yeah, yeah," I replied, not in the mood for small talk.

"You startin' a Fight Club in Crystal Palace?" he asked. "Sign me up."

I hobbled to my desk. Anne had left me another desperate answer-phone message. I now had a lot more information about her cheating husband than she may have wanted to hear. With trepidation, I hit redial. As the phone rang, I wondered how she might react to the news and whether I should even tell her. Within a split second of that thought I reminded myself that I was obliged to tell her. She had paid to know everything.

"Morning, Anne. It's Joe. Is now a good time to talk?"

"Joe, thanks for calling back," she said. "I was just putting the rubbish out, but yes I can talk."

"I have some news," I said.

"Umm. Okay," she said apprehensively.

"Before I tell you what I've found. I've got a question," I said. "The letter to Bill was signed from Dani, wasn't it?"

"Yes."

"What was it about the letter that made you think it was from a woman?"

"What do you mean? It's obviously a private letter from a woman. Why?" she asked anxiously.

"Well, it might be best if we meet to talk about this in person."

"No. I need to know now. Tell me please, Joe," she insisted.

"Well... I believe Bill is in a relationship with a man. A man, called Dani," I said slowly.

"What? I don't... That can't be true," she said. "What makes you say that?"

"I saw Bill in a bar last night with a man. They were holding hands."

"No. You must be mistaken."

At that moment Greg stepped out of the office and mouthed something to me. I held the palm of my hand over the receiver mouthpiece.

"I'll come and see you in a minute," I whispered.

"I need you in my office now," he said sternly.

"Excuse me?" Anne said on the other end of the phone.

I nodded to Greg.

"Sorry, Anne. I have to go," I said feeling torn.

"You can't just tell me my husband is running around with another man and then hang up. I paid you to give me proof. Do you have proof?" she said sharply.

"Not yet. Sorry Anne," I said.

Greg was next to my desk tapping his foot on the floor and holding his hands on his hips.

"I really have to go. I'll call you back in a moment."

"Don't you dare hang up on *me*." she said with a raised voice.

"Sorry. Just one minute and I'll call you right back. Goodbye Anne," I said and put the phone down.

"Mr .Sharma's on my line. He's pissed off that you haven't called him," Greg said. "And so am I."

"Sorry. I've been busy with -" I started.

"Drop everything else, Joe. Speak with him and arrange a meeting."

Greg walked me into his office and pointed at his telephone, which was off the hook. I picked it up.

"Hello Mr. Sharma, this is Joe."

"What kept you?" Mr. Sharma said gruffly, with an Indian accent.

"Sorry about the wait."

"I want to meet you at King's Cross railway station at midday," he demanded.

"Today?" I asked. Greg looked sternly again at me.

"Yes. Is there a problem?" he asked.

"It's eleven now. Can we make it twelve fifteen please?"

"Sure, why not. Buy three copies of The Times newspaper from the WH Smith newsagent in the main concourse. I'll be watching for you," he said and hung up.

I put the receiver down in a daze.

"What happened to you?" Greg said, looking at me from head to toe. "You look a mess. Get yourself together, Joe. I need you at your best. This case is important."

"Yes, of course I will," I muttered.

"I hope you have at least read the file?" Greg continued with his line of questioning.

"Most of it," I said, praying there would be no follow up questions.

The truth was I had barely opened it. Just then Greg's telephone rang and he lifted the receiver. He'd clearly lost interest in our conversation and dismissed me with a wave of his hand. He sat back at his desk and continued talking on the phone, so I made for the door.

Questions were spinning in my head; who was Mr. Sharma? What had I agreed to do? I only had a short time to try to find some answers. I returned to my desk, spun the combination lock on my filing cabinet and dug out the file. I pushed the half empty mugs of cold coffee and piles of paperwork to one side, pulled the file out and opened it properly for the first time.

Conscious of time, I flicked through what Greg had put together to get the basic facts of the case. My telephone rang, but I ignored it.

A photograph of an Indian girl was paper-clipped to the top of the first page. I recognised her as the girl in the newspaper, but the file had a different picture. Her name was Dipa Sharma. She was a young looking six year old. Turning the page I read that Dipa was Mr. Sharma's niece. I remembered from the newspaper that she had been missing for a couple of days. Mr. Sharma was going to pay handsomely, £50,000 to be exact, if we found her. That explained Greg's eagerness to pursue the case so aggressively. For him it was all about the money. For me, it was about reuniting a broken family.

Details of the last known location were provided, but that was all there was. Details on the rest of the family along with details of Dipa's friends and any recently made acquaintances had been left blank.

I arrived at King's Cross tube station with minutes to spare after the usual delays on the London underground. I ran up the escalator and fought through the crowds. I handed over a crisp ten pound note in WH Smith for three copies of The Times. I held the papers to my upper torso for all to see and walked out the shop while I looked for anyone who might have been watching me.

"Afternoon, Joe," a short man said as he stepped out from the crowd.

"Afternoon, Mr. Sharma," I said.

"I'm not Mr. Sharma, but I'll take you to him."

"Okay. Where are we going?"

"There's a car outside. Please follow me."

I followed the mysterious man to the front of the train station where a dark blue BMW 7-series was parked. Nice car. Two people were already inside, the driver and another man, lounging in the back seat with his arm draped over the headrest of the middle seat.

"Please sit in the back," the short man said.

He opened the door and the man in the back reached forward with an open right hand.

"Afternoon, Joe. I'm Mukhtar Sharma," he said.

I sat in the car and shook his hand. He was an Indian man in his mid thirties, well groomed with a neat goatee and a stylish suit with expensive looking black leather shoes. He tilted his head and looked at me with sly brown eyes as he placed his mobile phone in the back pocket of the driver's seat.

"Good to meet you," I said.

"Let's go for a drive while we talk," said Mukhtar.

The short man closed the door and walked off. The driver started the engine and we moved into the traffic. Mukhtar opened a packet of mints and threw one into his mouth.

"Before we begin, I need to know that you can be discreet. Are you a discreet person, Joe?"

"Yes, sir. My livelihood depends on it. I deal with sensitive issues for a range of clients on a daily basis," I said, feeling a simple yes would not suffice.

"Good. I want complete discretion, understand?"

I nodded, feeling uneasy as we continued to drive through central London. The young driver paid no attention to the bizarre discussion in the back of the car as he continued along the road, never once glancing at me in the rear-view mirror.

"You're not to tell anybody of your work for me. Not even your wife, Jennifer."

I felt threatened that he knew my wife's name and was about to ask the driver to stop the car, when I remembered Greg's warning to me. I decided to remain seated and listen a little longer. No harm could come from that, I thought.

"Okay," I said.

"Good, because Greg recommended you personally. I've filled in your paperwork. Do you have any questions?"

"Can you please talk me through the details of Dipa's last known whereabouts?" I asked.

"I provided everything I know to Greg," he said.

"I noticed some of the information we request on the forms was missing..."

"You don't need it. It's irrelevant," he said out of hand.

I know that relatives in Mr. Sharma's situation can be abrasive due to the trauma and worry of losing a loved one; I tried to remember that he didn't know if he would ever see his niece again or what had happened to her.

"I need to know as much as possible to help find her," I explained.

"You have everything you need already," he snapped. "We will meet next Thursday at the same newsagent at 1pm. I expect you to have made progress by then. My brother and I are relying on you."

"How can I reach you if I have further questions?"

"No need. We will meet next Thursday. Clear?"

"Yes, fine."

Mr. Sharma tapped the driver on the shoulder. The car pulled over to the curve. I stepped out onto an unfamiliar side street and they sped off. The clouds above looked threatening. It was blustery. Fast food wrappers tumbled down the empty street and it looked like it was going to rain.

I was mystified by Mr. Sharma's attitude and the secrecy of the meeting. He seemed almost unwilling to help me find Dipa. This was very unusual for a missing person case, particularly given the press interest. Relatives were normally all too eager to spread the word in the hope that someone, anyone, could help locate their loved one.

I recalled that horrible moment in the bathroom during my commute home that evening. Poor Stu. The anguish I felt from Stu's fear of me was nothing short of self-loathing. I felt a mix of guilt and sorrow in the pit of my stomach. I needed to tell him how much I loved him, to make it all better. I also knew Jennifer would be furious. Stu would probably tell her everything, which would not help my case, although I deserved it.

I opened the front door and stepped in. I could smell and hear the sound of sizzling stir fry. It occurred to me that I might have to cook my own dinner tonight. I took my shoes and coat off and headed into the kitchen to face the music.

"What the hell happened to the door?" Jennifer blurted out, while tipping a packet of bean sprouts into the pan. She didn't even look round at me.

"Good evening to you too. Sorry about that."

"Sorry? Stu is distraught. What happened?"

"Where is he?"

"Upstairs in his room, afraid of his own father."

I walked out of the kitchen.

"Leave him alone Joe," Jennifer yelled after me.

I ignored her and continued, upstairs. The bathroom door opposite Stu's bedroom caught my eye. The damage looked worse than I remembered. Splinters of wood were strewn across the corridor. I knocked on Stu's door. There was no answer. I tried to open the door, but something was pushed up against it on the other side.

"Stu. I just wanted..." I said softly.

"Go away," he yelled sharply.

"I'm sorry, Stu."

I tried repeatedly to speak with him, to convince him how sorry I was and how awful I felt. Nothing. I returned downstairs dejected. Jennifer was just dishing up. She filled one plate only. I wasn't hungry anyway.

"It's not working... us," she said with trepidation, as she took out a fork from the cutlery drawer.

A shiver went down my spine. I knew this conversation was coming. In fact it was overdue, but it didn't make it any easier. I had almost convinced myself it was just a bad patch in our marriage, that it would all be fine eventually. I certainly never wanted it to end. Despite her apparent resentment towards me, I loved her just as much as I ever had and would fight for her love again.

"No," I said.

"I think it's time to..."

"What?" I asked.

"... move on Joe" she said and walked into the sitting room with her plate of steaming food.

"You mean give up?" I said as I followed her into the other room.

"I've put everything into this marriage."

"And I haven't?" I said as I stood opposite her.

"You run around all hours of the day, giving no thought to me," she said while finally looking at my face.

"I work hard for this family."

She said nothing and stared at the floor.

"I love you. You need to say exactly what you expect from me," I said.

"Do I need to spell it out for you?"

"Yes you do," I said, calling her bluff.

She looked squarely into my eyes, "I want a divorce, Joe."

I felt those words like a blow to my soul. My wife and the mother of my only son wanted to leave me. It was so much worse because she was so confident and determined about it. Jennifer always did have a certain bloody-mindedness about her.

"I love you, Jennifer," I repeated.

"That makes everything cool then, doesn't it?" she said sarcastically.

"Is there someone else?" I instinctively asked.

She looked me in the eyes again, "Maybe."

"Who?" I demanded, "how long has it been going on for?"

She turned away to put her plate on the sitting room table. I was mad. I grabbed a mug from the table and threw it hard at the wall. Smash. Shards of porcelain scattered across the room and dregs of coffee splattered against the whitewashed wall.

Jennifer ducked and covered her head, dropping her plate of stir fry onto the cream carpet. The plate bounced on the floor and the vegetables and rice drenched in sweet chilly sauce splattered across the floor and up the lower half of Jennifer's light blue trousers.

"What's wrong with you?" she yelled, while stepping over the mess to get away from me.

"I won't let you divorce me." I yelled and stormed into the foyer. I was not going to be trampled over.

I needed to get away, to have space to think. I stopped myself from leaving straight away, as I considered the possibilities. I would need food later so I went to the kitchen pantry and grabbed a couple of packets of biscuits and four cans of beer. I also took some bananas from the fruit bowl and an apple. I put the food into my work rucksack and took my car keys from the shelf in the hall. Everything else could wait. I needed to get out. Jennifer peered round the sitting room door as I slammed the front door behind me, hoping to break another.

Four

I drove away like a maniac, revving the 1.5 litre engine as I raced the car along the darkened narrow streets of my neighbourhood, between the parked cars on both sides. I didn't give a damn. I was quite happy to take my frustrations out on the car's tyres.

"Divorce! Screw her," I screamed aloud.

Ahead on the road through the darkness I made out an opened car door and someone's leg emerging from a vehicle. There was no space to swerve around the open door, so I slammed my brakes on and skidded loudly along the tarmac. My work bag, which I'd placed on the passenger seat, hit the dashboard hard and fell to the floor. My seatbelt locked me in a brace, as my eyes widened.

I came to a stop feet from the open car door. My headlights illuminated the wincing face of the poor woman who was stepping out of her car. She froze to the spot for a couple of seconds. She sat back in her seat and pulled the door closed quickly.

I pulled away calmly and drove onwards at a sensible speed. I kept driving for a while, trying to get away from the London lights, till I came to Wimbledon Common. I pulled into a small car park and turned the engine off, which made a series of clicks as it cooled.

Outside, the woods were silent and still. It was a dark and cold April night. Without the car headlights, I could barely make out the trees. The occasional car travelling on the road behind me cast fast moving shadows of the branches that danced across the tree trunks in front of me. Kinda spooky. I hit the car central locking button and turned on the internal light.

The car was usually a complete mess with empty cereal bar wrappers and half empty plastic water bottles on the floor, but it was my salvation. I had sat in that car on countless cold nights during surveillance jobs, watching and waiting outside hotels, casinos, theatres and cinemas. My car contained everything I needed. I turned to the back seat and felt around: binoculars, torch, notebook, pillow, umbrella, petrol can, newspapers, radio. The familiar soft fabric of my blanket brushed my wandering hand. I pulled it close and wrapped it around my legs and waist.

Hunger pangs soon sprung upon me. I reached to the passenger seat well and tipped the contents onto the seat. Biscuits, fruit and some paperwork rolled out. I savagely ripped open the first pack of ginger nut biscuits and stuffed some into my mouth. Not exactly appetising, but I was used to such improvised dinners. I washed them down with a beer. I grabbed my insulin pen from the glovebox and dialed in ten units before injecting myself in the stomach. It always hurt.

I turned on the car radio, conscious not to have it on for too long for fear of having a flat battery in the morning, a mistake I had made once before on a job.

I flicked between radio stations, till I found some easy listening music. With nothing else to do, I shuffled the paperwork among the food. A phone bill and a life insurance policy leaflet.

Out of boredom I found myself reading through the policy small print. *'The policy is invalid if death results from a pre-existing medical condition or in the event of suicide.'* I took a swig of beer and stared into the darkness.

I decided it was sensible to apply for a policy, given I had no savings set aside for Stu, so nothing to pass on to him. I filled in the paperwork in the dim light. I opted for a sizeable payment in the event of my death, out of guilt for not spending much time with him. The premium was steep but Stu was worth it. Hell, he deserved some security. I sealed the prepaid envelope containing the completed form. I felt pleased to have achieved something positive that evening.

I finished another beer and started my third. I was cold and tired, so reached for my pillow from the back seat. A distant light appeared, it was another car, but this one slowed and turned into the car park. Glancing at the side mirror I could see that it was a police car. Great. I threw the empty beer cans on the floor and pretended to be asleep.

I heard the vehicle stop and a door open. Footsteps came to my car door and then there was a tap on my side window.

"Evening, Sir," a policeman said as he lit me up with his torch beam.

"Evening, Officer," I said as I opened my eyes.

"Can I ask what you are doing, Sir?" the policeman said.

"Umm. I was sleeping."

"Sir, have you been drinking?"

"Umm. Yes I've had three beers. I wasn't going to drive anywhere though."

"Is this your vehicle?" he asked.

"Yes."

"Can I see your driving licence please?"

I reached into the glovebox and handed my papers over.

"I'm sleeping here tonight because I had an argument with my wife. I have nowhere else to go," I said honestly.

"Sorry Sir. The law is quite clear. You cannot drink and sit in a motor vehicle with the keys. Step out of the vehicle please."

I did as asked and closed the car door. "I wasn't going to drive anywhere," I repeated.

The officer took something out of his holster. "Please blow into the breathalyser, Sir," the officer looked on as I blew into a plastic tube. "Keep blowing, keep blowing and stop."

He turned and nodded to his colleague sat in the police car, who opened his door and stepped out.

"Please place your hands together, Sir, behind your back. You're under arrest..."

"What? I've done nothing," I insisted.

"You do not have to say anything, but anything you say..."

"Okay. Arrest me. Why not. I'll probably have a better night sleep in a cell anyway."

The truth was that I spent a large part of the night replaying the conversation with Jennifer in my head, interrupted only by random football chants bellowed out by a lout in the next cell along. His favourite for some reason seemed to be, "he's big, he's red, his feet stick out the bed, Peter Crouch, Peter Crouch."

The next morning I forgot where I was for a split second and expected to be at home, till I saw an unfamiliar white wall and realised the bed was much harder than usual. My heart sank. I had nowhere to go. I was incarcerated. A prisoner of Her Majesty's.

"Shit."

I uncurled my body from the narrow bench and stretched out. My feet kicked the wall. The cell was too short for me. I turned over and tried to go back to sleep.

"Morning Sir," a jolly voice boomed out.

The door thumped open. I jumped up.

"How's the head today?" the PC asked.

"Okay thanks, but the bed is a tad uncomfortable."

"It's not great in here, is it? The good news is that the sun is shining and after some paperwork and a fine, you'll be free to go."

I reminded the officer as diplomatically as I could that I was not the usual drunk driver, in fact I was no danger to anyone sat in my stationery car. This did not have the desired effect, as I was verbally harassed by the officer on the dangers of drink driving for an hour before finally settling the hefty fine with a credit card.

"I'm late for work. How can I get back to my car?" I asked, once our business was concluded.

"One of my colleagues will drop you off."

Police Constable Kelly volunteered to drop me. However, on the way we were diverted to assist a road traffic accident involving a motor bike and a lorry. You can guess which driver came off worse. I could hardly complain about the delay as sat in the backseat of the police car, watching the motorcyclist being stretchered away by paramedics.

Once back in the woods at my car the first thing I did was to throw my remaining beers into a ditch. I then hurried to work and sneaked through the door at one in the afternoon. My run of bad luck failed to change though, as I met Greg in the corridor.

"Hi. Sorry I'm late," I said.

"A word, please" Greg ordered, as he waved me towards his office. He closed the door and turned to look at me.

"What's happening? Your work is slipping."

"Sorry. Personal problems. I know I've been sloppy recently. It won't happen again."

"One of your clients called today and made a formal complaint against you. Anne Close. She said you called her to say her husband is gay, then apparently hung up on her and didn't call her back to explain."

"Oh god," I held my head.

"She was in tears and spent twenty minutes going over her bloody sob story."

"Sorry Greg," I said. I knew she would have taken the opportunity to jabber on to Greg, which would not have helped my case.

"I haven't got time to pick up your pieces. Just sort her out, then sort yourself out. Okay?!"

I spent the next half of the day speaking with Anne Close, first on the telephone and then at a trendy coffee house near her London home. I turned on the sympathy, aware that Greg expected me to leave a happy customer.

Over three cups of coffee, I apologised at length for leaving her hanging and sensitively laid out the evidence as I saw it for why I thought her husband was having an affair with a man. I held back on nothing, even giving her the password to her husband's e-mail account and advising her how best to check it in the future.

"Thanks Joe," she finally offered.

"I wish I could have said everything was alright. I really do," I said, continuing the charm offensive.

"I feel like a fool. I never saw the obvious," she said.

We both sipped our coffees in silence. The cafe was empty of all other customers. The shop owner was scrubbing the floor behind the counter, trying to keep busy.

"Are you married?" Anne asked.

"Yes, for the moment... she's pushing for a divorce," I volunteered.

"Oh, is that what you want?"

"Well, maybe it is" I revealed, more to myself than Anne.

Five

It was a bleak Wednesday morning and my next meeting with Mr. Sharma was only a day way. I had at this point done little to progress the search for Dipa, because of the many distractions in my life. Greg was pissed, so I decided to pull out all the stops to find little Dipa. I opened the file, took out her smiling portrait and stuck it to my desk shelf for inspiration. That poor child was out there somewhere.

After rereading the limited information that Mr. Sharma had provided, I made a list of what was known about Dipa's disappearance. She was last seen outside King's Cross underground with her mother at 13:30, almost two weeks ago. Her mother had lost her in the crowd. Given her age, six, and the duration of her disappearance, Dipa's ultimate fate was most likely sinister.

I was familiar with statistics from missing people cases. Around 300,000 men and women are reported missing each year in the UK. Most of these people are between the ages of 15 to 17. The next biggest demographic is between 18 to 30 year olds. The number of missing children under the age of 8 is small.

Adults disappear for a range of reasons, but usually because they choose to run away or have a mental disorder. Young children do not generally choose to disappear, most are abducted or abandoned. Family abductions are the most common type of abduction, and also the most obvious to solve. The police normally locate a child within a few days if they are abducted by a family member.

Given the length of time of her disappearance, I suspected that she had not been abducted by a family member. The police should have found her by now if she had been. Statistics indicate that most abducted children that are murdered, tend to be dead within the first few hours. I feared Dipa may already be dead, but had to assume she wasn't.

To make sure I wasn't missing anything obvious, I typed 'Dipa Sharma' into an internet search engine and read a range of newspaper articles. The police were apparently interviewing some suspects, but had no solid leads. It was clear that her parents were fully engaged with the police investigation and had done a couple of press conferences. This confused me, because Mukhtar Sharma had insisted on being discrete, while Dipa's parents had seized every opportunity to publicise her disappearance.

Armed with some nuggets of potentially useful information, I grabbed a coffee and hit the phones, to reach out to some of my professional contacts. I needed help to break the case open and a good PI has a network of paid sources who can get answers to the difficult questions you can't answer yourself.

It had taken me a few years to build up such a network, because it usually meant they 'acquired' information from their day job and passed it to me, which meant they risked being discovered and losing their jobs. For this reason, most of my sources never wanted anybody to know that they were working for me, so welcomed covert meetings in private locations. This was not as glamorous as you may think, meeting in dull libraries and grubby pubs.

One source of mine was Gareth, a receptionist at a hotel. I paid him to locate any guest who had stayed at any hotel in the countrywide chain he worked for. For a little extra he would even throw in the credit card details that the guest used, if they were still on the booking system.

Gareth, like my other contacts, knew he was risking his job and even a prison sentence whenever he agreed to work for me. If the money was not worth the risk then he would not do it, so I paid him accordingly. However, something more was required than just money; Gareth had to trust that I would keep the information safe and not misuse what he had provided. That sort of trust was built up slowly over months of working with a source.

I prided myself on maintaining the trust of some very influential people who worked for me. As well as Gareth, I had contacts in two major banks, a mobile telecommunications company, the UK Border Force, a local library, TV licence office and even a policeman. I also found it useful to remain friendly with several journalists who had their own range of contacts.

My most prized contact was Dan, who worked at the local council. He had a wealth of information at his fingertips, from the names of individuals who had paid council tax, to historical UK census facts that were not public knowledge. Dan had a large family and always welcomed the chance to earn some extra money to spend on his five children.

Dan was not very risk averse: we met on weekly basis to do business, either in a pub during the week, or otherwise on a Sunday morning at Crystal Palace lake, because we were both members of the Crystal Palace Angling Association and whiled away the hours catching perch and roach and talking shop. I thought of him more as a business partner than a source, because I'd worked with him for so long.

I called Dan and gave Dipa's and Mukhtar's details over the telephone. We arranged to meet that evening in The Red Lion. I always bought the drinks.

"Evening. You alright?" I asked Dan, as I approached him in the corner of the pub, with two beers in hand.

Dan was a thick set guy, bigger than me. He always wore the same dull orange t-shirt, which I'm certain he never washed, given his horrific body odour. He had matching tattoos of intertwined stars on his thickset forearms.

"Abbey's pregnant again," he mumbled.

"Congratulations, mate."

"Err. I had a vasectomy last year, remember?" he said.

I nodded vaguely, but truthfully I couldn't keep track of all the twists in Dan's soap opera personal life.

"So," he continued, "either she's cheated on me again, or the bloody surgeon cut the wrong tubes!"

"Well..."

"All that pain, for what? My balls killed," he squirmed.

"Sorry Dan." I smirked. "What are you going to do?"

"God knows," he said and took a large gulp of beer. "Anyway, how's you? You look like shit."

"In a world of pain. I got hit by a mark the other day, but what's more painful is Jennifer's having an affair and wants a divorce."

"Wow. I'm sorry mate. Here I am jabbering on..."

"No, it's fine. I just need somewhere to live."

"Well I would let you stay over, but my house is fillin' up fast."

"I'll be fine. It's just come out the blue."

"To women," Dan toasted, raising his glass, "screwin' with our lives in every way possible." We clinked glasses and took some gulps.

"By the way, I've got some info on that Dipa Sharma," he said as he took a thick sealed brown envelope from the seat next to him and slid it to the centre of the table.

"Excellent. What did you find?"

"British, with Indian parents. She's lived in three London homes during her life. Interestingly, Social Services have a file on your Dipa..." he took a gulp, "Her arm was broken suspiciously, and she had bruises..."

"Family violence?"

"Social Services couldn't prove it."

"Good work, Dan. Did you find anything on her uncle, Mr. Mukhtar Sharma?"

"Nope. There's nothing on him. It's as if he doesn't exist. But, for completeness, I've printed off what I've got on Dipa's dad, Advik," Dan said as he patted the envelope.

After one last drink, we went our separate ways. I was excited about what could be gleaned from the contents of the envelope, so decided to burn the night oil. I walked back to the deserted office, let myself in and sat at my desk, still with my winter coat on because the heating had turned off.

I opened the envelope to find two files, one labelled by Dan as 'Missing Girl' and another labelled 'The Dad'. I set aside 'The Dad' file and flicked through Dipa's first. I was impressed to see that Dan had included photocopies of the original Social Services reports, which detailed the investigation into young Dipa's broken arm. The doctor's diagnosis was that her arm had been broken in two locations, consistent with two forceful blows to her mid and upper humerus.

Social Services had tried to interview Dipa, but she refused to speak with them and so they had been unable to ascertain from her what, or who, had caused the fractures. Dipa's parents had insisted that she had simply fallen down concrete stairs. Social Services had started a file on the parents but no further action had been taken.

I kept going through the papers, but by the early hours of the morning the text was blurring before my eyes. At about the same time I became aware of the smell of burning dust from my desk lamp. I turned it off, leaving myself in pitch blackness, and rested my head on my arms on the desktop. Within minutes I was asleep.

It was bitterly cold when I woke up. I was shivering and my toes were numb. I raised my head slowly from the desk and felt a pain in my neck, from sleeping awkwardly. My body always ached when I slept at my desk. I fumbled for the lamp switch in the pitch black, turned it on and saw that it was ten past five. I stood and stretched.

I took my spare toothbrush out of the drawer and wandered through to the kitchenette to freshen up. I returned a few minutes later with a clean face and a hot coffee. It was rather out of character for me, but in the short time since I'd woken, I had already found the conviction to begin a productive working day, despite still wearing yesterday's clothes.

Satisfied that I'd teased out the valuable information from Dipa's file, I started on Advik's file. I read through some council tax records. He paid his taxes annually. Boring. I flicked through the census records. Equally boring. Dipa's school records were next. Hang on. It seemed that Dipa went to Cranley Primary School, which was also Stu's school. That was odd.

There was no mention in Advik's file of any siblings. Dan appeared to be right, Mukhtar didn't exist. The Mr. Sharma I knew was not Mr. Sharma. I felt conflicted. I needed to focus on keeping the client happy, but the client had lied to me and I was curious what his motives were. I decided to focus on the job. Greg was already exasperated with me and would kick off if I caused him any more bother.

Later that day, I walked into the WH Smith newsagent at King's Cross at the agreed time. I waited expectantly for someone to approach me, as before.

"Hello again," a voice came from behind me. I turned to see 'Mr. Sharma'.

"Hi," I said, "what happened to your entourage?"

"No need for them today. Let's walk."

He strutted ahead of me out of the shop. I followed as he quickly crossed the station concourse and out of a side exit onto the street. He stopped with no warning at the next street corner, allowing me to catch up with him.

"Have you found anything useful yet?" he asked as he turned to face me.

"I'm... making progress," I said, recovering my breath from the quick walk.

"Do you know where Dipa is?"

"Not yet. I'm still waiting for some leads that should narrow the search area," I said. "Can I ask what the police have told you?"

"I need you to keep diggin'," he said, brushing off my question. "Investigate Theo Mistry, who was sentenced in November 2007 for burglary. Tell the police everything you dig up on him. Theo Mistry, got it?"

"Theo Mistry." I said, pulling out my pocket notepad and pencil to scribble the details. "Okay. Don't you want to tell the police yourself?"

"No, it's better coming from you. You'll tell them. Understand?" he insisted.

"Why don't you want to tell the police yourself?" I persisted.

"You need to stop asking questions and start doin' your job."

I bit my tongue as I resisted the temptation to ask 'Mr. Sharma' who he really was. I'd pushed my luck enough and needed to rein it in.

"Okay. I understand."

"I expect you to have found her by next week. Meet me at the same time and place."

He turned and walked briskly down the street. I waited a second, considered whether to follow him and then thought better of it. Curiosity would have to wait, as any further test of Greg's patience would likely end badly.

Six

I text Jennifer on my way back to the office to tell her I would pick Stu up from after school club later. Some father-son bonding time was exactly what I needed, especially as I had not seen Stu since frightening him. I needed to meet him on neutral ground to apologise properly.

Jennifer failed to reply to my text, but I left work when the time came and commuted back to my car, before driving to school. I parked up round the corner and walked to wait with the other parents outside the school gate. I recognised most of the parents, but had never had any meaningful conversations with any of them.

There were a few flowers woven into the chain link fence here and there along the perimeter. Some of them had little messages stuck with sticky tape next to them. The note nearest me, which was clearly written by a child, read *'Dipa, I miss you and want to see you soon. Sophie.'*

I walked a bit further to the gate, making my way sensitively through the crowd of unusually quiet parents. One woman had tears running down her face as she looked at the ground. I came to the notice board and read the details of the poster with Dipa's photograph, which simply stated *'The thoughts of all staff at Cranley Primary School are with the family of Dipa Sharma at this time. We will of course set aside time during the school day to offer counselling to any children who need help dealing with this sad news. Please let us know if your child has been particularly affected.'*

The bell rang and Stu was one of the first to the front gate.

"Hey Stu. How was your day?" I asked.

"Not good. Can we go?"

"Sure. What's wrong?" I asked as I tried to cuddle him, but he pulled away.

"Dad! I don't like cuddles," he reminded me.

"Sorry. Let's walk to the car."

"Do you know Dipa?" I asked.

"Yes," he said, but offered nothing else in reply.

"I'm sorry Stu. It's really horrible she's gone missing," I said, "were you guys friends?"

"We played sometimes," he said, kicking a stone.

"Is that why you didn't want to go to school the other morning?" I asked.

He nodded and I instantly felt like the worst dad on the planet. I hadn't listened to him and just assumed that he was skiving some test or avoiding a homework deadline.

"Let's go home," I said and rubbed his back, as we strolled round the corner to the car, "I'm sorry about the other day. I didn't mean to frighten you."

He nodded again, still looking ahead.

"Are you and Mum going to stop fighting?"

"I hope so Stu."

I opened the door to the backseat and Stu hopped in.

"I love you," I said as I looked at him through the rear-view mirror.

"I love you too, Dad," he said, staring back at me with a broad smile.

It was a relief to make up with Stu. I knew it would not be so easy with Jennifer. We got home to an empty house. I opened an envelope addressed to me on the doormat, which gave my life insurance policy details. I left the open letter on the kitchen table, thinking it was a sensible place for it to be discovered by Jennifer.

Stu and I played with remote control cars, racing them around the living room. I nipped into the kitchen briefly to put on some dinner for him before rejoining the fun.

"Can I ask you about Dipa?" I said, as Stu's car overtook mine, only to glance off the skirting board and take a spin.

"I guess," Stu shrugged.

"You see, I'm helping to find her. It would be great if you could tell me anything you know that may help get her?"

Stu knew I was a private investigator. I like to think that he bragged about his old man with his friends. I had never told him anything specific about my work though, just in case the details turned into playground gossip. This was different, Stu may have known something that the police didn't.

"A policeman came to my class yesterday and asked the same thing... I didn't want to say anything though, in case I got in trouble."

"You won't be in any trouble Stu," I said, kneeling down to his level. "We all just want to find her. That's all. Do you think you know anything that may help?"

"I don't know... She really likes school, which is weird."

"That's good. What about home?"

"She gets in trouble a lot," Stu said.

"Did she ever get hurt?"

"Yeah, ages ago. Her Dad hit her."

We heard the front door slam.

"Mum?" Stu yelled and ran out of the room, still holding his remote control.

I sighed in anticipation of the tension between Jennifer and myself. I walked into the hallway to see that Stu had greeted her warmly with his arms wrapped around her waist. She placed her coat on the usual hook in the hallway.

"Good day?" I asked, with a forced smile.

She walked right by me into the kitchen, not even acknowledging my presence.

"Stuart, what do you want for dinner sweetheart?" she asked with a singsong voice.

"I've put on fishfingers and chips," I said, following her into the kitchen.

"He needs vegetables," she said curtly.

I shrugged my shoulders, "I'm trying everything. I don't know what else I can do."

"Not now. Not in front of Stu," she said.

"I feel like you have banished me from our home. I haven't slept here for days."

"Stop it Joe," she said in a raised voice.

"Dad? Mum?" Stu said.

As I had foreseen, the atmosphere was unbearable.

"Maybe you're right. It might be better just to end it," I said. I had had enough of grovelling to her and being treated like a child. I turned and walked back to the hallway.

"What's wrong with Dad?" I heard Stu ask Jennifer.

"Don't worry sweetie," Jennifer said, "stay here while Mum and Dad have a talk, okay."

I stood by the front door, weighing up whether I could sleep in the car again, stick around at home, or go somewhere else. Jennifer stepped out of the kitchen, closed the door and put her hands on her hips.

"Pull yourself together, Joe," she whispered. "I've got a lawyer and he's preparing divorce papers. You need a lawyer too."

"On what grounds are you divorcing me? I've always provided for you and don't hit you," I quipped, not wanting to make it easy for her.

"Try, never being here for me, for Stu," she said bitterly. "For buggering off to see your stupid *friends* every night of the week, which apparently you can't even do right either."

"What?" I asked, "what did you say?"

"You're the PI, Joe. Work it out," she spat.

I couldn't tolerate her tirade anymore. I turned the handle of the front door and left.

"Go on, run away as usual," she yelled bitterly. I pretended not to have heard this final taunt.

My head was swirling with feelings of hate and anger for Jennifer, and guilt for leaving Stu. I couldn't bring myself to sleep another night in my uncomfortable car, so drove down the road to a cheap hotel. I had no luggage and no clean clothes. I walked through the sliding glass doors into the empty lobby and towards a keen looking teenager who stood tall at the reception desk, dressed in an ironed red shirt embroidered with the hotel logo. Two minutes later I was in a room which came with uninterrupted blissfulness, compared with being at home anyway. It was, in reality, a small room with the basic mod cons, peeling wallpaper and en suite complete with an odour of mould.

I was lathing my hair with the hotel supplied shampoo when it hit me that Jennifer may have been having an affair with Greg. Greg had been avoiding me recently and only he had known that I had been struggling at work. I leaned against the tiled shower wall and gasped. I was a bloody idiot. It all seemed to make sense. I felt sick.

I had a restless night running over and over what Jennifer had said to me. I didn't know what to do. I paced the room in the dark muttering wild thoughts to myself, cursing them both for being so devious. I figured I had no choice but to continue working for Greg. There was nothing else I could do. Then I doubted myself. What if I was wrong? Maybe I had jumped to the wrong conclusion?

When my alarm rang in the morning I peeled my eyes open. Lack of sleep was becoming the norm. I decided that morning to play it cool till either of them confessed, or till I had proof.

On the way into the office I stood once again in the cold on the station platform, transfixed by a fresh billboard poster which advertised a tropical drink, set on a perfect beach. I wanted to be there, to be far away in the warmth. I needed to escape my life.

Thankfully Greg was not at work that morning. I had nothing to say to anyone else, so kept a low profile. To keep my mind distracted I kept working on the Dipa case. I started by calling my police contact to look into the lead I had been handed on a silver platter from my slippery customer 'Mr. Sharma'.

"Hi Thomas, it's Joe. What's new?" I said on the phone.

"Joe. Four months to go until my pension kicks in," he gloated.

Thomas was a Detective Superintendant in the Metropolitan Police Service, with decades of experience in the area of violent crime. He loved a juicy murder and thankfully for me he was a bent copper who also loved money. He was arrogant as hell, but it was worth putting up with his attitude to get access to some great information.

"What you goin' to do when you retire?"

"Well, I'm considering taking up an offer to become an advisor to the Dubai Police Force."

"Lots of sun, sand and, I'm sure it pays well," I said.

"Yeah. Well, I'm sure you didn't call to offer advice on my future career prospects. What can I do for you?"

"Same arrangement as usual," I said cryptically over the phone.

"Yes, fine," he confirmed, without missing a beat.

"Theo Mistry. I don't know where he lives."

"Any further info? You could get the phone book."

"Sentenced for burglary in November 2007. Possibly linked to that girl who went missing, Dipa Sharma. That's all I've got."

"I'll see what I can do. Let's meet at four today."

"Great. Usual place," I confirmed.

Click. The line went dead. I usually met him in Hyde Park on a certain bench and we always kept meetings brief, so we were together for only a short time.

I had almost four hours to kill at work before I had to leave for the rendezvous. My computer pinged to life with a new e-mail. I turned to the screen and opened the message from Greg entitled 're: Expenses'. Inside was a reply to one of my expense claims, with a single comment against a soft drink, which read 'I can't justify this payment'.

He had the nerve to decline the one pint of Coke I had bought while waiting for Bill Close in the pub the week before. It was no great pleasure sitting in that pub and then getting hit in the face. My blood boiled. I was furious. I hit reply and typed the first thing that entered my head.

'Go to hell. I'm not taking any more of your shit. I know you're sleeping with my wife. I want to kill you!'

My mouse pointer hovered over the send button on the screen. I pressed gently on the mouse, willing myself to send it. I paused, deleted the last sentence about killing him and then hit send.

"Sod it," I said aloud.

I pushed the keyboard and mouse away in disgust. What had I done? So much for playing it cool. I'd been completely stupid. I tapped the desk quickly with my fingers.

"What's wrong Joe? Are you alright?" Alice asked, popping her head round the corner.

"Sorry. Everything's fine. It's just my stupid computer."

"Tell me about it. Bill Gates is a criminal."

"Yeah," I said while my brain whirred into life. I had a flash of genius and jumped up, "is Greg out all morning?"

"He's in Birmingham for some meetings," Alice answered.

"Excellent. I'll use his computer."

I walked swiftly into his room, closed the door and turned on his computer. I had seen Greg scribble passwords down in the back of his diary some months before and hoped his computer password was there. I still had a chance to save my job, but had to be quick to gain access to his e-mail account before he read my message on his phone.

Seven

I opened Greg's top desk drawer. Inside was an A5 sized envelope containing a couple of thousand pounds. I set it aside and kept looking. Underneath was his desk diary, which I flicked through. I froze when I came to what was obviously his computer username and password on the back cover. Even professionals get lazy with their passwords.

Once Greg's login page appeared on the screen I furiously typed in his username and the password, which was *'Jen.4ever'*. I hit enter in disgust.

His e-mail page opened and at the top was my unopened message. I deleted it and also purged it from the Deleted folder. Next I glanced down the e-mails in his Inbox for anything from Jennifer, but nothing jumped out at me. That said, they would both have been pretty stupid to have exchanged e-mails from Jennifer's usual e-mail account, since Jennifer knew I had her password and could have checked if I ever had any suspicions.

I kept looking through Greg's Inbox and found a message from "seeyousoon123@hotmail.com". I clicked on the message. There were several pages of gushing romantic drivel. I scrolled down and found that it was signed from *'Your Jennifer'*. My heart sank. My suspicions had been confirmed.

I couldn't stand to read it, so hit the back button to the Inbox. I decided to try and find the first message from that address, so ran a search. Six months ago. The devious bitch.

I cancelled the search, returned to the Inbox and was about to log out when I noticed a message from 'M.Sharma@gmail.com', which I decided was worth a look. I opened it and read: 'G, it was good to see you again the other day. As agreed, let me know who I can deal with. M.'

It was weird that he had used initials instead of names in his message, but I already knew 'Mr. Sharma' had something to hide. I logged out, turned Greg's computer off and stepped away from the desk. I found myself staring into space. The question of the moment was, what should I do next?

The worst thing about my predicament was that it affected my home and work life, both components were teetering on the brink of annihilation. The PI community in London is a tight, but fickle group who love gossip. If the truth got out then the rumours would flourish and ruin my credibility as a bonafide PI. How could I pick through clues into others' affairs when I couldn't even see an affair much closer to home.

I left the office early to get some air and arrived at Hyde Park over an hour before I was due to meet Thomas the policeman. I strolled around the park to ensure no one had followed me, which gave me a lot of thinking time.

I couldn't afford to let my feelings get out of control again. It had almost cost me my job. I had to be cool and logical. I decided to investigate 'Mr. Mukhtar Sharma' for starters, as Greg had obviously met him on multiple occasions. My gut told me that there was some dirt to be dug up on him. I hoped that some of that dirt would stick to Greg.

I decided to follow Mukhtar next time we met. I knew this would be a difficult task. A normal surveillance operation required multiple people who rotated to take the lead, to ensure the target doesn't see the same person following them if they are looking. I would need a plan and a disguise, as Mukhtar knew what I looked like, and while my face maybe forgettable, I couldn't rely on that alone.

I hadn't seen anybody following me during my random meanderings through the park, so sat on the usual bench. Thankfully it was a dry and mild day, but Thomas arrived in his usual trench coat. The idiot looked like a spy wannabe. I knew from experience that his attire was simply to hide his police uniform. I had warned him before about meeting me in public wearing his uniform, but he was too lazy to change first. It was more convenient for him to come straight from work.

"Afternoon," I said, as he walked towards me carrying a briefcase and a racquet.

"I'm playing squash at four thirty, so let's be quick," Thomas said as he sat.

He twisted the combination dials on his briefcase, clicked it open and laid the case on his lap. He pulled out an envelope and handed it to me.

"Thanks Tom. What did you find?"

"It's all in there. I don't have time to talk today," he snapped and waved his hand at me for payment.

He was an arrogant git who assumed his senior police status commanded my respect. He overlooked the fact that if his employers ever became aware of our business arrangements, his illustrious career would be over without the plush pension he was so close to claiming.

"I'm not going to pay you till I know what you've given me," I told him, as I opened the envelope.

"How dare you test *me.*"

"Shut up Tom. If the Police had done their job properly, Dipa would be back with her family already," I said, tired of his attitude.

"Just give me my money Joe," Thomas ordered. He leaned across and tried to snatch the envelope back from me, but I pulled it out of his reach. "Give me the envelope."

"Did I ever tell you how my brother was killed?" I said calmly.

"What?" he said, screwing up his face.

"He was walking across a road when a speeding unmarked police car hit him and threw him in the air."

"I don't care," Thomas said coldly.

"Both his ankles, a leg, hip and his arms were broken, along with his neck. He was paralysed, but he didn't die from the impact. No, he died on the pavement about two minutes later when he choked on his own blood, while your colleagues" I said poking him hard in the ribs, "drove on."

"Go to hell Joe," Thomas said as he stood and stormed off.

I could have stopped him and apologised, but I didn't want to. Bloody police. I didn't trust any of them.

I had begun to accept that everything was changing. My life was in a downward spiral. I knew that would be the last time I saw Thomas. I smiled. I hoped the envelope contained something useful. I peeled it open in trepidation. It contained a couple of photocopied papers about Theo, the man who Mukhtar had tipped me to investigate.

According to the police records, Theo lived in Surrey, in a small village called Shere. He had history; theft when he was a teenager, assault, for which he spent twenty months in prison and most recently in 2010 he was connected to a human trafficking ring, although never formally charged. Then there was the burglary charge that Mukhtar had already told me about. Theo was a dual national, holding both a British and Greek passport and formerly resided in Malta. He looked older than he should, as he had completely white hair, even though he was just thirty eight.

I had never dealt with any human trafficking cases. I wondered how, in this modern world, criminals could get away with kidnapping and holding people against their will for sustained periods of time. Selling people was simply barbaric. Maybe the mysterious Mukhtar had stumbled across a genuine lead. Theo needed investigating quickly. I truly hoped he would lead to Dipa, but time was slipping away.

I folded the papers, stashed them into my rucksack and headed back to Hyde Park tube station. I needed to pick up some equipment to set up a surveillance operation. Time was running out for Dipa and me. I had one day left before my next meeting with Mukhtar.

During the cramped underground ride back to London Bridge, I squeezed into a seat and daydreamed about a better life. I had visited Malta as a boy with my parents. It was a peaceful place with a laidback way of life. That was the life I wanted, to settle down in one place and open a small shop or even better, a pub. Something on the beach, where my patrons could unwind with a drink in their hand, looking out at the sea. I always found that I slept so much better after spending time near the sea, I think it is something about the salty air or the rhythmical soothing sound of the waves. I longed for a decent nights sleep.

After some further research back at my desk, it turned out that Theo lived in a farm just outside Shere. He was clearly in the money, to afford a farm in Surrey.

Aerial photography of the plot showed the farm included several outbuildings and the main farmhouse. There were no neighbours within half a mile, which meant it was going to be difficult to get close without raising suspicions.

The standoff distance was considerable, as there was little cover nearby. I needed some kit so I didn't have to get to close to the buildings. I knew just the woman to help and she was just a short walk from my desk. I popped through to the front office to speak with the company surveillance expert, Alice.

"Hey Alice, I need your help please."

Alice stopped typing and turned in her chair. "Well, do you need my brains or hardware?" she said playfully.

"Umm. Your hardware, every time. I'm just that sort of bloke."

"You and every other red-blooded male on this planet," she retorted. "So, tell me what you need then?"

"I'm planning a surveillance job and really need to borrow your camera and a telescopic lens, please?"

Technically the equipment belonged to the company, but Alice was the only person who used it. She had taught me how to use the camera once, when I showed an interest during a slow week.

"I could come and help if you want?" she offered.

"Thanks, but I want to do this one myself."

"How long do you need it for?" she asked.

"Two days tops. I'll get it back to you by the end of the week?"

"Well, you're in luck. I don't need it at the mom. Just be sure you don't break it and remember to recharge the batteries afterwards."

"Awesome. You're the best Alice."

She went to the store room at the back of the office, unlocked the door and turned the lights on. I followed her into the cramped room and was hit with a strong and tangy smell of new plastic, The sort of whiff I usually associate with most products made in China. These fumes probably emanated from the boxes of equipment and other clutter that lay on the array of shelves. Alice searched a couple of boxes before finding one of her large telephoto lenses. With both hands she carefully passed it to me.

"It's worth four grand. If you drop it, I'll drop you off the Shard. Got it?" she warned.

"Alright. Don't stress."

The lens caps were on, so I placed it carefully on the floor outside. She found the camera in its bag along with the charged batteries. I saw some camouflage netting in the corner, so grabbed it for good measure. That would give me good cover while I hid in the copse near the buildings.

"Thanks, Alice."

"What about an image intensifier?" she offered.

"What does that do?" I asked in wonder.

Alice picked up a strange device that looked like a monocular, with a handle and a trigger.

"It lets you see in the dark. It's a Russian military unit. You just squeeze the trigger to activate it."

I checked out all of the gear back at my desk, reminding myself of the camera settings, before wrapping it and the lens inside some plain plastic bags for protection against the wet. The image intensifier was great fun, when you peered through the eyepiece and pressed the trigger the room came to life. Unlike in the movies, I didn't blind myself when I used it in the bright room, the viewing screen just went white. I chuckled at the thought of trying it in the pitch dark.

I placed all the new toys inside my rucksack, which was bulging. I left everything I didn't need, namely the instructions and camera case, on my desk. I was about to leave when the picture of Dipa caught my eye, so took it from my desk and slipped it inside my wallet.

I dropped by my home on the way to Shere to collect some more basic tactical gear, namely food and clothing. It would be cold later that night and I was going to be exposed to the elements.

Eight

The sky was black as I drove through the country lanes and past a sign that read *'Welcome to Shere'*. The air was crisp and with no clouds in the sky I knew it was going to get colder, probably with ground frost. I deliberately drove straight by the farm to sneak a peek to see if anyone was home. I could barely see some lights inside the house, but couldn't make out any other details because it was set down a winding unlit track, back from the road.

I turned off onto a side lane after a short drive. The lane had deep ruts from farm traffic, but had clearly not been used in a couple of years because the foliage had reclaimed the area. I drove only as far as to be certain no one could see the car from the road and pulled the handbrake up.

Before leaving the warmth of the car I put on two jumpers, a winter coat, hat, boots and gloves. I grabbed the camouflage netting, plastic ground sheet and my rucksack. It now contained a large bottle of water, torch, the camera gear, note pad and pen, biscuits and two self heating food tins, one beef hot pot and one chicken curry. I knew from bitter experience that they both tasted pretty horrible, but were a convenient way of getting a warm meal.

I closed the car door quietly and turned on my torch, keeping the beam angled down. I made my way through the shrubs onto the farmland. There were no crops in the field and it looked like the earth had recently been ploughed. My feet sank deeply into the loose mud as I walked, which hindered progress. I hadn't anticipated getting so mucky. I should've brought my wellies.

The farmhouse was beyond the next hedgerow, so I worked my way slowly along the edge of the field till I found a gap big enough to look through. It was a perfect place to be positioned, with a view of the back of the farmhouse and two of the three outbuildings. I threw down the ground sheet onto the uneven grass that was sprouting beyond the reach of the farmer's plough and opened my rucksack. I organised what I needed onto the sheet. I threw the camouflage netting over the top of my back, both for visual cover and extra insulation from the cold.

I took out the image intensifier and surveyed the farm buildings through the viewfinder. There were warm areas by the windows and doors of the main house. I glanced up and even saw heat from the chimney, so there must have been a fire on the hearth below. I could clearly see the lights were on in all the rooms downstairs, apart from one with a small window, which was most likely the toilet.

There was movement across the windows on occasion. It was difficult to be sure how many people were inside, but the shadows were quite tall. I estimated three or four adults.

It got colder as I lay there watching the sky fill with beautiful stars. My eyes adjusted to the dimness and could even make out the Milky Way twisting overhead like a path of shimmering dust.

Looking around through the viewfinder, I was surprised to see an area of warmth under the door of the small barn. It was a faint heat source compared to the heat coming from the main building, but something was there. The barn had no windows, so I couldn't see inside.

Suddenly a bright spot darted across my view through the image intensifier. I pulled the eyepiece away from my eye and saw a cat ran past the barn towards the farmhouse. I shivered and took a deep breath. Water vapour from my breath floated upwards into the air.

The cat scratched at the farmhouse backdoor. I raised the image intensifier again. A silhouetted figure of a man appeared at the door, his torso and head glowed brightly. He could've been Theo Mistry or my postman for all I could tell though, it was just too dark to see with my eyes and the infrared image on the viewfinder was unrecognisable. Whoever he was, he held a dull coloured object in one hand, which seemed to be shaped like a pistol, but I couldn't be sure. He stared out into the darkness for a few seconds, with two orange coloured pits where his eyes were positioned.

He looked down at his feet as the cat pounced inside, into the dark green coloured warmth of the house. He then stepped out of the house and held the object in his hand exactly like a gun. It was a gun.

"Bloody hell," I whispered.

The farmhouse was about fifty metres away. I was confident he couldn't see me, but at that moment I realised the sort of serious characters I was investigating. I held my breath as he casually walked to the barn with the dim light under the door. He put his free hand on the door handle, presumably to check it was locked, and then meandered back to the main house and disappeared behind the closed door. Phew.

I relaxed and put the image intensifier on the ground. My eyes were sore from the effort of staring at the small screen. There must have been something important in the outbuilding. I needed a closer look, but it could still have been dangerous, so I had to wait a while.

Later, I blindly fumbled about in the dark for my rucksack and eventually found one of my meals inside. I wanted to minimise any use of the torch, just in case someone was looking out of the window. I pierced the food canister with the sharp metallic tool provided and left it to warm by itself. I couldn't read what flavour meal was cooking, but I didn't really care. I left it to the side of the ground sheet and tried to relax.

I noticed some of the lights on the ground floor had been switched off while others on the first floor were now on. I was distracted by the vague smell of curry, which lay to rest my curiosity about what I would be eating.

Remembering my doctor's instructions, I took out my insulin injection, lifted the many layers of clothes I wore and injected myself in my exposed fatty stomach. I couldn't see the dial properly so guessed my dose, which he wouldn't have approved of, but what harm could it do if I was a bit off?

I found a fork in the dark, but then had to turn my torch on to open the top of the can to eat. I turned to face the field, so as to hide the light from view of the farmhouse. I scoffed my food quickly. It was far from satisfying, but did have the desired warming effect.

I ate two biscuits while considering the dangers that lurked in the farmhouse, with slight trepidation. No one knew I was in that field, which in hindsight was pretty stupid. No one would have known if I had been killed by those criminals. My mobile had no reception either, being in the middle of the country.

I accepted the risk, but wanted to take one precaution, to write a letter to my Stu. Should the worst happen that night I wanted to leave him with a message from me. I took out my pen and paper pad and wrote a letter for my son.

'My Dear Stu,

Just in case anything ever happens to me, I want you to know that I have left everything I own to you. You are the most important person in my world.

Whatever you choose for yourself in life, make sure you stay true to yourself and be happy. Happiness is sometimes stolen from you by others, but you must fight for it.

Whatever you hear about me from others, please remember I have always loved you.

All my love.

Your Dad. Xxxxx'

I finished the letter under the mist of my breath, folded the paper and put it inside my rucksack. I turned off the torch and spun myself around to see that the farmhouse was in darkness.

At two in the morning a deep frost had gripped the field. I'd dozed off for a while, but was satisfied that everyone in the house was asleep. There'd been no movement in the darkened windows, so thought everyone was asleep. I decided the time for waiting had passed.

I piled the camouflage netting to one side and stood slowly. This was painful after lying still for so long, as the cold made my joints ache. I pulled together all the equipment, while being in what I thought was a foggy daze caused by my nap. I headed back to the car. I walked quickly to help wake up and keep warm. The muddy field was now solid with ground frost, making the mud crunch underfoot.

I put Stu's letter in the glovebox, as it would be more likely to be found in the car, if I had got caught. I placed the equipment in the boot, so I could make a quick getaway if needed. Finally I grabbed my trusty crowbar.

I locked the car quietly and set off. The adrenaline had kicked in at this point. I took deep lungfuls of fresh air as I retraced my footsteps through the field to the gap in the hedge that had been my hideout for the last few hours. I stood there shivering, more from fear than cold. I had to look inside that barn. I hoped to find Dipa or at least a clue to her disappearance.

The lights were all still out, so I squeezed gently through the hedge and brushed the ice from some of the leaves with my jacket. I instinctively started to jog to the barn but started to wheeze, so changed to a fast walk.

Suddenly I was gripped by an implausible fear, that someone would spring out of the farmhouse and run the short distance to intercept me, wielding a gun. I recognised that this fear was borne from tiredness and not rational thought. Normally the more exhausted I became, the more irrational my thoughts were. I reminded myself of the facts: The lights were off and no one had stepped out of the farmhouse for several hours.

I re-focussed on reaching the barn door. I knocked and waited pensively for a response, ready with the crowbar raised above my head. There was nothing but silence; no one was inside.

I dropped to the floor to look through the crack underneath. I couldn't see anything and I'd left the image intensifier in the car. I pulled myself up to my knees and turned my torch on to examine the best way to open the two heavy duty locks, which were flush against the wood at both the sides as well as the top. There were no nooks to lever the crowbar against.

'Shit.' I muttered.

I sank to the floor again in disappointment. I noticed that the floor underneath the door was concrete and the wooden door was weathered at the base. I slotted the crowbar underneath and jammed it in as far as possible.

I rose to my feet and looked around again. I pushed my body against the crowbar. The door creaked slightly and some of the paint at the base flaked off under the pressure. A few splinters flew into the air.

I grabbed a stick lying nearby and as I forced the door with the crowbar it curved outwards and I jammed the stick into a crack that appeared at the side of the door. I then removed the crowbar and reinserted it next to the stick at the side of the door. I now had excellent leverage halfway up the door. I stood and stepped back slightly. With a raised foot, I gently bounced against the end of the crowbar. The door creaked again, but was tougher to move this time.

This was annoying. It was taking longer than I had wished. I raised my foot again and this time kicked the end of the crowbar. The bottom half of the door panel crashed outwards. My heart jumped to my mouth. I grabbed the crowbar and ran to the side of the barn, where I hid from view of the farmhouse.

I put my head round the corner and was relieved to see that all the farmhouse lights were still off and the bottom of the barn door was now hanging out, broken just below the first lock. I waited a further minute for any activity, but there was none so returned to study the damage. The gap was not quite big enough for me to squeeze under, so I gripped the broken panel tightly to pull it outwards.

I winced as something dug through my glove and into the palm of my left hand. I pulled my hand back to see a large splinter sticking up, with blood flowing from the centre. I carefully pinched the wooden sliver with my other hand and extracted it. A shooting pain went through my hand.

A pool of blood quickly formed in my palm, dripping to the ground. My blood was also spattered on the edge of the door. I peeled off my woollen glove, turned it inside out and pressed it against the wound, which stemmed the bleeding.

The adrenaline coursing through my body ensured I refocused my immediate task. I squeezed the glove into the wound and pushed myself through the hole into the barn.

Nine

There was a foul smell in the air, like rotten meat. I scanned the room with the dim torchlight. The barn floor space was about ten metres square and five high. I could just make out thick and gnarly wooden rafters crisscrossing above. The floor had an ultra smooth concrete screed finish, which must have replaced original straw or dirt.

A light switch was positioned next to the entrance, but I didn't dare flick it on as this would have almost certainly have been visible through the broken door. I decided to stick with the more discreet torchlight, which meant there were thick shadows constantly jumping around the room, which added to the creepy atmosphere.

A bench with clutter on it was situated next to the door. I stepped closer and saw lots of small multi-shaped strips of white photographic paper that littered the worktop. At the centre of this mess lay a scalpel on a rubber graphic design cutting matt. There was also a colour printer on the bench, connected to a laptop computer and numerous passports on the side, with more visible on a shelf above the bench.

I glanced down; there was a small wastepaper basket under the bench which contained a plastic bag with scraps of photographic paper, including several cut up photographs. I did not have time to rummage through the bin, so took the entire plastic bag out of the basket, tied it up and squashed it inside a jacket pocket.

Next I picked up one of the passports on the bench. I knew it wasn't British, but didn't recognise the nationality. I opened it and saw a name, Gavin Whittaker, and date of birth, 2 August 1977. There was no photograph present on the page, just an empty white box. The passport looked accurate and the security features looked genuine. The front cover had embossed print with the right feel, stiffness and stitching at the spine. It was too dark to have a proper look, but if it was a forgery then it was a really good one; really high quality. I slipped the incomplete passport into my jacket pocket.

I picked up four other passports from the shelf and flicked through them. Two contained photographs of young girls and the third was seemingly owned by a middle aged man. The passports on the shelf were complete, while the ones on the bench were still being prepared. I put four further passports into my pocket too. I wanted evidence from the scene for Mukhtar and, ultimately, the police.

There was a single piece of paper stuck on the wall with a Maltese address typed on it. I did not know the significance so made a note of the address in my notepad. I glanced across the room and saw a white screen and a stool. I guessed that was where the passport photographs were taken. I thought that this seemed to be a slick and well organised illegal passport factory. There was serious long term investment here and if found, this sort of crime came with a lengthy prison sentence.

Still concerned for my own security, I went back to look out of the narrow entrance in the door. There were still no lights on in the farmhouse. It was three in the morning. My fear turned to excitement. I seemed to have found something big. It was unclear how Dipa fitted into this murky world though.

I explored further into the barn, to find where the rancid smell was emanating. I followed the concrete floor along the wall, passed the bench and photo area and came to a large rectangular white box. It was a large deep freezer, which hummed to life as I approached. I jumped and my heart skipped a beat.

I gripped the handle and paused before pulling the bulky door upwards to open the freezer. The internal light came on and illuminated a large area of the barn. It was a bright light, which hurt my eyes, after being in the dark for so long. I squinted, which helped. I glanced into the freezer to see that it was empty. Thank God for that, I thought.

I left the freezer door open, as the light was far stronger than my torch and did not fall in the direction of the door. I saw the large barn space far more clearly. There were two other cabinets on the far wall, a bath and a strange long parcel on a sheet.

I followed the beam of light across the barn and noticed the strange package was wrapped up in sheets. The smell got stronger as I got closer. The parcel became clearer and looked more and more like a body wrapped in cloth. There was definitely a head end, with the largest width just below that, which looked like shoulders. The other end tapered out to the feet. I could see the toes through the fabric, which were bloated. The body seemed to be a man, who was about six foot or so, although it was hard to estimate, as he was just lying there in the partial darkness.

The hairs on the back of my neck stood to attention. I didn't dare go any further forward. My pulse raised and I backed away to the door, but continued to stare at him. I never saw the man's face, but he couldn't still be alive, not with that stench and bloated state of the feet.

I wondered whether he had been killed recently or not. I didn't know how quickly the human body decomposed. I guessed it must be a day or so before that smell develops.

I walked towards the freezer and closed the lid. In hindsight I don't know why I did this, as the light went out and left me in near total darkness again. I stumbled back to the door, glancing back at the 'mummy' once or twice more as I made my way out.

I glanced across and saw a single light turn on in the farmhouse, on the second floor. Shit. I sprinted towards the gap in the hedge, while turning off my torch. I only had seconds to escape, so didn't even duck to go through the gap in the hedge, but simply ran through it, taking some of the branches with me.

My arms and legs pumped and lungs burned in the cold. I hadn't run so fast since the fifty yard dash at the school sports day twenty years earlier. My head began to hurt. I glanced behind me to see some lights were now on at the lower level. I kept going through the field and the second hedge.

I stopped to look back once I was behind the second hedgerow. I heard raised foreign voices shouting aggressively. There was a man leaning out of the window on the top floor and the door opened with another man stepping outside. I was hidden in the inky darkness, but was worried about the hedge I'd destroyed, which would put them on the right path to find me. No one had started to follow me yet, so I still had time.

I turned and tried to run again, but instantly felt sick and gagged. I had to stop as I heaved from the exertion. I felt really light headed. Bloody hell. My vision became fuzzy. I forgot what direction to go. I had to keep moving, but leaned my hands on my knees to support my bodyweight as I staggered forward a few steps, but it was all too much. I tripped and fell into a shallow ditch.

My sense of reality warped further. My field of view narrowed. It felt like I was experiencing what diabetics call a hypo, or hypoglycaemia, which is low blood sugar levels. I'd eaten food though, which meant I must of taken too much insulin earlier, when I couldn't see the dial properly.

I struggled to undo the zip on my coat, with numb fingers. I fumbled inside my inner pocket and took out a packet of glucose tablets, but it was too late. I forgot what I was doing, felt even more faint before resting my head on the ice-covered earth.

I woke in the dark and cold, lying on my front, with a splitting headache and a dry mouth. I tasted mud on my lips, which I wiped with my sleeve. With a struggle, I pushed myself up onto my arms, out of the mud. I felt weak and tired.

I tapped my fingers on the earth around me for the torch, but couldn't find it. My glow-in-the-dark watch showed me it was five in the morning. I had to get moving, but couldn't tell where I was. I stood and looked around. There was a glimmer of daylight beyond the horizon. I got my bearings and pushed on, towards my car.

It was a miracle that the men hadn't found me. I opened the car door, climbed in and collapsed. I felt safe inside the locked car, so closed my eyes for a while. I glanced at myself in the rear-view mirror. I had a small gash in my forehead and dried blood smeared down my face, mixed with mud on my chin and neck.

I touched the gash and winced. My head throbbed again, like I had a bad hangover. I was more beaten up than a demolition derby car. I ate some biscuits and began to feel better. A cockerel called out, as the sun was about to rise. It was time to move. I started the engine and reversed out of the side lane onto the country lane.

I didn't initially care whether I was heading the correct way home. I just needed to get space between myself and the men in the farm. I headed away into the country. I drove for twenty minutes down winding lanes, before starting my GPS and setting it for home.

Several hours later I was home alone. Jennifer was at work and Stu at school. I had a couple of hours before the next meeting with Mukhtar. I showered, redressed and unpacked. I searched my mud encrusted jacket for my mobile phone. I tipped the contents of the rucksack onto the bed and frantically searched through the stuff. It wasn't there. I remembered last having it at the stakeout, in my coat pocket. I checked the car, but it hadn't dropped out in there.

It could have fallen out when I collapsed on the ground. I was worried because I knew how easy it was to identify someone from a mobile. I also knew those men wouldn't risk leaving me. I was clearly a liability to their illegal ambitions.

I had to assume the worst; that the men had found my phone and were already working to identify and locate me. It wasn't safe to be in the house, as my address was linked to my mobile account. I had to leave straight away. Stu and Jennifer would also be in danger. A hundred other thoughts raced through my head as I pulled together what I needed.

Should I go to the police now or wait to understand what I was mixed up in first? I had tainted experiences with the police in the past. I preferred to work through the problem myself. It was time to have a frank discussion with the one person who I was certain knew what was going on.

I grabbed my car keys and made for the door. I remembered the letter I wrote for Stu and ran back to the kitchen and placed it next to the toaster. Before opening the front door I peered down the street through a side window. There was the usual level of traffic. I couldn't see anybody waiting for me in a car but I had a limited vantage point.

I deliberately waited for the next pedestrian to come into view of the house, a young women pushing a pram. If someone wanted to shoot me on my own doorstep then there would at least be a witness. I opened the door, stepped out and slammed it as I ran to the car, using it as a shield. I started the engine as the mother passed the driveway and pulled away.

I turned hard right into the road and skidded off, while paying particular attention to my rear-view mirror. A navy blue car pulled out from the line of parked cars behind me. It seemed to be travelling fast and catching up. Chances were that it was just a neighbour in a hurry, but I took no chances. I revved the engine and remained in second gear as I accelerated to the upcoming right turn, taking it at thirty miles an hour.

The blue car also turned, as I continued at pace. I was still uncertain whether the car was following me or just going the same way, so I started a lap of the block. There was a red light ahead with a car stopped at it, so I slowed right down to five miles per hour but kept moving until the light went green, as the men behind were less likely to get out of their vehicle if I was still moving, however slowly I was travelling. The moment the car in front turned off, I accelerated again, round the next left corner.

A red car pulled in behind me and round the next corner a white van joined the convoy. It became harder to tell if the car was still behind the other vehicles. On the fourth leg of the lap I caught a glimpse of the blue car coming round the corner behind the van and car.

I took the next right and raced through a red light, manoeuvring between two moving cars on the crossroad. They braked and honked madly, but I ignored them as well as most of the UK traffic laws. Next, I turned down a one way street, going the wrong way, like a good car chase from any film, all the time trying to eliminate the line of sight between me and my pursuers as much as possible.

I came to a side road and saw a space between two parked cars. I braked hard and pulled in. I turned the engine off, hunkered down in my seat and waited, breathless. I topped up my blood sugar with a banana while observing my surroundings, using only the car mirrors. I was confident that I'd lost my tail so climbed out of the car.

I saw a payphone on the corner of the street, some thirty metres away. I had to warn Jennifer and Stu as they would soon be heading home, possibly into a trap. Some cars passed down the side street, but the blue car was nowhere to be seen.

I opened the car door cautiously and headed to the phone box, looking both ways down the street as I walked. I needed to keep my wits about me to stay alive. I took out some change from my pocket and dialled Jennifer's mobile, tapping impatiently at the phone box window as I waited for the connection.

"Jennifer, you need to listen to me," I blurted into the phone.

"Come on, Joe. This isn't the time."

"No. It's not what you think. Your life is in danger," I insisted.

"What are you talking about?" she asked.

"There are some men outside the house right now. They're there to kill us."

"I think you've been lost in your make-believe world too long, Joe."

"It's not safe to go home. I found a body last night and now they're after me," I garbled.

"What? Who?"

"You have to get Stu and go to your mother's. You can't go to work either at the moment. It's not safe. They'll find you."

"Is this some sick joke or your feeble attempt to win me back?"

"No. Please trust me, for Stu's sake," I said.

"Trust you to screw us up even more than you already have. This is the last straw Joe. You better sort this mess out. I don't ever want to see you again."

"You have to get Stu right now, while I find out what's going on," I begged.

Ten

I drove into central London because I wanted the security of having a getaway vehicle in case I needed to make another hasty exit. I made slow progress through the usual gridlock of traffic. I sat in lane, patiently inching forward and resisting the urge to break any further traffic laws.

I finally parked in an extortionately expensive multi-storey car park a short walk from King's Cross train station. I walked the rest of the way, only stopping to purchase a pay-as-you-go mobile phone from a small phone retailer.

I found myself standing outside the WH Smith in King's Cross train station, where Mukhtar had told me to meet him at the end of the previous meeting. By this time I was in no mood to play his games. I needed answers.

A short time later he swaggered towards me, with shades on and chewing gum. He clearly thought of himself as some sort of Mr. Big, despite his short stature.

"Solved the case yet?" he asked mockingly.

"I made a discovery about Theo Mistry," I said.

"Well, what have you got then?"

"Before I tell you, I want to know how you know him?"

"That's none of your business," he said defensively.

I had a hunch in that split second and decided to trust my gut instinct.

"What's your business?" I asked.

"I don't know what you are talking about. Theo is a family friend," he said, while glancing up and to his left.

I noted his eye direction, as one of my interests is simple physiological techniques, particularly Neuro Linguistic Programming, which teaches that when someone looks up and to the left when answering a question it tends to mean the person is accessing the artistic side of their brains. In short Mukhtar had just lied to me.

"Are you trying to get him put away?"

"Are you sure you want to piss me off? Remember who's working for who," he shouted and prodded his forefinger into my chest. His overreaction suggested I had hit a nerve.

"If you're a murderer too, then it would be a mistake," I said.

"Have you got proof that Theo killed someone?" he asked.

"There's a dead body at his farmhouse," I retorted.

"Have you told the Police?"

"Not yet. I wanted to tell you first."

"You need to tell the Police."

"Why don't you make the call?" I suggested.

"You saw the body, not me."

"Let's go to the nearest Police station right now and tell them together."

"No. I've got other appointments today, Joe."

"What can be more important than reporting a murder?" I pushed.

"You go," he said and walked off.

I saw red. Every event that had led to this moment, Jennifer and Greg deceiving me, Mukhtar treating me like a fool, my life falling apart, the murderers trying to kill me, even the bad London traffic, filled me with rage. I grabbed him from behind by his fancy leather jacket, spun him around and pushed him against the side of the shop, where I held him.

"Is it 'cos you're hiding something? I know Mukhtar Sharma isn't your real name," I said.

"Get your hands off me," he shouted, while squirming to get free.

I pushed him harder against the wall. I had the bodyweight to keep him planted. A couple of commuters turned their heads to look at the scuffle, but no one intervened.

"Your boss will hear about this," he spat.

"The body wasn't Dipa's by the way, since you forgot to ask. You never did care about her though, did you? Was it all about getting to Theo?" I shouted.

"Go screw yourself!"

I hit him in the ribs, hard. It felt good to knock the wind out of him.

"Get someone else to do your dirty work. I'm done," I said and let go of him. I turned and strode away, hoping he would think I wanted nothing more to do with him, which of course, wasn't entirely true.

I got to the other side of the main station area, glanced briefly over my shoulder through the crowd of commuters and spotted him still by the shop; realigning his coat and sunglasses. He was now my surveillance target. He walked across the concourse and was about to disappear through the front entrance of the station.

I jumped into action, walking quickly after him. Despite his cocky attitude, I suspected that he was quite alert and aware of his surroundings, so I had to be careful.

I took off my reversible coat, which was a useful tool of the trade, with interchangeable sides, either dark blue or grey. I turned it inside out and put it back on. I removed a baseball cap from a pocket and put it over my hair. A simple and effective disguise.

I reached a glass wall next to the main doors and stopped to peer through. The sunshine reflecting on the other side meant I couldn't be seen from the outside, which was handy in case he decided to wait in the street to catch sight of a tail.

I caught a glimpse of Mukhtar's silhouette jogging away down the road. He seemed to be more interested in fleeing the scene than ensuring no one was shadowing him. I ran through the station doors after him and crossed the road, to follow from a safe distance on the opposite pavement.

He stopped at a pedestrian crossing and walked across to my side of the road. I darted into a small corner shop and waited a couple of seconds in case he double-backed on himself. He didn't pass the shop, so I stepped outside carefully and headed down the road in pursuit again. Ahead of me a gleaming black BMW braked hard and pulled up alongside him. He opened the back door and dived in. The car squealed away. I raised my new camera phone and took a picture of the number plate.

I needed transport and quick, to keep the pursuit going. I flagged down a black London taxi, jumped in the back while still monitoring the car ahead through the cab windscreen.

"Follow that car," I said urgently.

"Really?" the middle-aged taxi driver asked sarcastically.

"Do it, now!" I yelled.

The driver sighed, but pulled away and began to catch up with it. The black BMW drove along at the speed limit, indicating where appropriate and obeying all road signs. My taxi was two cars back, which was the perfect place to guarantee discretion while tailing someone. The taxi driver concentrated on his task as we meandered the London side streets.

"I never thought I'd ever get to do this," the driver said. "Are you some sort of spy or undercover policeman?"

"No," I said simply. "Make sure there is always at least one car between us and that BMW. I don't want them to know that we're following them."

"Right you are, governor," he said. "If this is your job, I want to know where I can sign up. This is the most fun I've had in years."

I was in no mood to make small talk. I sat back and reflected on the madness that had occurred during the last week, as our little convoy passed Russell Square tube station.

I thought again about when and how to involve the police. I was convinced that they would be more hindrance than help to me if I approached them directly at this time, plus I just didn't trust them. I considered the possibility that the police could, however, be useful to investigate the dead body, if I could get the information to them anonymously.

I knew how the police tracked people as I employed the same methods myself. In the age where you leave your digital fingerprints everywhere, I had to be careful about how to ensure my message was truly anonymous. If I had called the police they could have tracked my mobile number and undoubtedly spent considerable effort trying to identify me. I needed a way to guarantee my security while providing the information they needed.

"Do you have a camera in this cab?" I asked.

"It's broken at the moment," my driver told me. "Why? Are you planning to rob me?" he smiled and glanced at me in the rear-view mirror.

"Don't worry. Can I give you a note to give to the police?" I asked.

"That sounds mysterious. I can take you to a police station if you want."

"No. I need someone else to drop it off for me."

"What?" he said, obviously confused.

"I'll pay you a hundred quid," I offered.

"Well in that case, fine! I'm your man. No questions asked."

I took out my small notepad and began to draft a note. It was difficult writing as we drove, as every bump and corner distorted my handwriting, which I'd been told was bad anyway. With concentration I managed to complete something which was vaguely legible.

The content of the note simply said I had found a body which was being hidden by armed men. I provided the address with a rough stretch map of the farmhouse, date and time the body was seen. I left the note unsigned, obviously.

I looked up as I finished the note and recognised the street we were driving along. A chill went down my spine as I realised I'd miscalculated Mukhtar's next step. We were only a street away from my office. He was going to see Greg, to complain about my behaviour. I'd hoped he would lead me to his house or someone else who might have been linked to the case, but instead it looked like all I had achieved was to stir up further trouble for myself.

"You can stop here," I told the driver.

"Okay, but we're going to lose him," he said as we pulled to the curve.

I ripped open the envelope of money I'd meant to give to my police contact Thomas, before he stormed out of Hyde Park the other day. I took out five crisp twenty pound notes and another to pay my bill. My cabbie turned to accept his prize, with a beaming smile.

"Thanks, you've made my day. That was fun," he said.

"Just please make sure the police get this note today," I insisted, pressing the folded paper into the palm of his hand.

"Sure. Don't you worry. I'll drop it off next."

"Thanks."

"You stay safe out there," he said genuinely.

Eleven

The black BMW was parked opposite my office. The chauffeur stood on the pavement beside the car, in a suit and jacket with his arms folded and staring at the front door to my office. I passed him and noticed there was no one in the back of the car, but the engine was still running. Mukhtar had obviously planned to leave quickly. Greg's car was also parked out front in his usual space, with the number plate 'GRG1'. The arrogance. I set my nerves aside and strolled through the front door as nonchalantly as I could muster.

The front desk was vacant. I heard raised voices from the main office next door and stepped through the door to investigate. Greg stood with his arms crossed at the side of the room, while Mukhtar had his back to me and leaned against my desk. There was no one else in the office. They were deep in discussion and so didn't notice I was there.

"I hold you accountable if he ruins anything!" Mukhtar shouted, "our entire operation could be jeopardised if he discovers..."

"He's not going to. I told him to *stick to the girl*," Greg said.

I took a step back out of the main office and hid behind the doorframe, where I could earwig their conversation without being seen.

"Well, clearly he isn't. If you can't control your staff then maybe I should manage our business at the warehouses?" Mukhtar said threateningly.

"That has *nothing* to do with this," Greg said.

"You better hope so," Mukhtar said.

I heard the front door click closed and turned to see Alice and Ben.

"Hi, Joe," Alice called.

I waved at them, saying nothing. The talking paused next door. Greg and Mukhtar must have heard her. I rolled my eyes to the ceiling. Alice had blown my cover. I walked through into the main office again in a nonchalant manner. Greg caught sight of me this time, raised his eyebrows and sidestepped Mr. Sharma.

"Joe. A word now." he ordered.

"Yes, sure." I volunteered, feeling like a sacrificial lamb.

I accepted my fate and instinctively knew the meeting would not end well for me. Greg led me into his office. Mukhtar followed, fuming with rage. We all stood in Greg's side office, with them facing me. Mukhtar stepped forward into my personal space and gave me the eyeball.

"There's something wrong with you, punk. You assault me in public and then have the nerve to follow me," he said. "What's your problem?"

Ben and Alice came through into the main office. Greg pressed his door closed to shut out them out.

"I didn't follow you. I work here," I said.

"What's with the new jacket and cap then?" he asked.

I fell silent, unprepared to answer. Some people thrive in pressure situations, but not me. When they say fight or flight, I choose flight every time. The problem was that I was always too slow to think of that perfect reply during the heat of the moment. I also had the habit of torturing myself after any dispute by replaying key moments over and over in my head to formulate the ideal response, which achieved nothing.

"Joe," Greg said, "you've disappointed me again with your lack of professionalism."

I said nothing, but wish I'd said "I couldn't give a damn if I *disappoint* you." I had lost all respect for my boss and mentor. I stared him in the eyes.

"What the hell do you want me to say?" I asked rhetorically of the two people I preferred never to speak with again. "I investigated the case of a missing girl. It soon became clear that *Mukhtar* here was hiding something."

"You don't have a clue," Mukhtar said.

"I know you're name's not even Mr. Sharma."

"You don't know anything," he said.

"My job is to find the truth, however uncomfortable it is."

"Shut it, you bloody Boy Scout," Mukhtar blurted.

"You're nothing more than a common criminal using a missing child to get revenge on a competitor. How else do you explain your strange behaviour and the lead you gave me that took me to a dead body?" I said staring at Mukhtar with distain.

"I don't care about your wild theories. You better be a light sleeper, Joe, 'cos you'll be getting a visit soon. No one screws with *me*. Understand?" he threatened.

He calmly opened the door and strolled out, leaving me in a state of shock. Without any hint of regret or interest, Greg walked to his desk, sat down and logged onto his computer.

"You can go now. Let's talk later. I've got work to do," Greg said.

"So, you have nothing to say to me?" I asked.

"Yes, I've got a lot to say, but not right now," Greg said.

"You don't care that my life is in danger? People are trying to kill me 'cos of a job you gave me, or was that always the plan to get me out of the way so you and Jennifer can live happily ever after?"

"Joe. Don't do anything rash," he said still with his fingers on his keyboard. "We have known each other for a long time. I know that Jennifer makes things a little strange but we can..."

"I quit," I interrupted him and walked out of the office leaving the door open.

He didn't try to stop me. I expect he was probably relieved that I'd quit, as it saved him the trouble of firing me. Alice and Ben stood just outside his office and gawked as I walked towards them. I struggled to keep my feelings contained, so said nothing as I continued out of the door and into the next chapter of my life.

As I walked away from the office, my job and a large portion of my former life, I knew it would be tough, but I felt strangely driven to prove something to myself, Jennifer and most of all Stu. I wanted Stu to be proud of his father. The last few months had been nothing less than a complete mess. I feared he must have been losing faith in his old man. I needed to show him I could rise above everything that had been thrown at me.

I was acutely aware that I had no safety net now. I was alone, so had to be smart and agile. I walked to Waterloo to get on the tube. I had to recover my car.

It was 4:30pm and the train carriages had begun to swell with tired people heading home. I felt safe on the underground because of all of the CCTV cameras, but someone could have been following me. I made my way to the northern line, going north, but jumped out at Leicester Square, walked between platforms and got on a Piccadilly Line train to King's Cross.

While I sat on the moving tube carriage, bouncing slightly in my seat, I thought about the snippet of conversation I'd overheard between Mukhtar and Greg. It seemed that Mukhtar was not a client of Greg's, but a business partner and they had some sort of warehouse business. They'd both lied to me, but I still didn't know why.

I looked around for anyone who might have been following. This was difficult given the number of people in the carriage. No one seemed to be taking an interest in me. I was mindful though that while most people avoid acknowledging anybody else on a train in London, a trained surveillance officer would do the same.

At Russell Square I jumped off the tube, while minding the gap, ran up the escalators and walked briskly to the nearby National Hospital for Neurology & Neurosurgery. After entering the hospital I headed straight up the staircase to the second floor before coming straight back down to the ground floor by lift and back out of the building via a different door. This was for no other reason than ensuring that I hadn't been followed.

As I reached the car park, I stopped on the pavement and turned to scan for any familiar faces in the street from earlier in my journey. I recognised nobody and so was completely satisfied that I was safe.

I was mindful of the possibility that my car could have been found hours previously and they could have been lying in wait for me on the level where I was parked. I decided the risk was manageable as long as I moved safely and kept my eyes open. I held back from entering the multi-storey car park till a young couple headed towards the side door. They were holding hands and wistfully oblivious to me as I followed in haste. The smell of stale urine burned the back of my nose as we climbed the concrete staircase together. I was parked on level three, but the couple continued to level four, so I followed.

They walked to their blue Renault Clio as I headed to the down ramp. No one else was around on that level. As I peered between the concrete to the floor below, I stood in a small pool of oil, probably from a sump leak. I saw no one loitering below. I edged down the side of the ramp to level three. I heard the couple's car start, so deliberately moved to the middle of the road, forcing their car to slow and follow me. Their presence guaranteed my safety. The killers wouldn't want witnesses if they wanted to kill me.

The car horn beeped as the headlights threw a long shadow of my physique onto the far wall. I feigned a drunken disposition by swaying slightly and waved in a friendly manner to the male driver behind me as I remained in the centre of the road. I continued slowly ahead, guided by their headlights inside the otherwise dim concrete structure. The down ramp on that level was just after my car, which was parked ahead on the right by the ticket machine.

Another car appeared from the up ramp, ahead of me. I stood still in the road. The driver behind beeped a longer tone and their electric window whirred down.

"Get out the road," the man said.

I swayed a little again, but needed to see who was driving the car ahead before I walked to my car and let them pass. An old lady was behind the wheel. She was short, with a blue rinse and wore thick glasses. I like to think that the only assumption I made about my safety that day was that the old lady was not a trained assassin. I quickly stepped aside to the ticket machine and started to pay my ticket. A squeal of tyres echoed around the building as the couple in the car behind me sped off. I jumped and dropped a twenty pence piece on the ground.

I ducked down and picked it up. As I stood I glanced down the length of the car park and saw a man wearing a thick winter coat with a hat and sunglasses walk from the doors at the other end. I walked straight out in front of the old lady's car and waved her down. She braked hard and stopped inches from my legs. I took a deep breath and looked at my leg as I imagined the pain I would have felt if she had been a little slower to stop.

I moved to the side of her car and waved her to open her window. She instantly pressed the central locking button on her dashboard and started to pull away again. I stepped back in front of the car again and she braked once again, this time making contact with my leg, which bent slightly, but not painfully.

"I just wanted to say that I am leaving if you want my space. You can have my space," I yelled at her, trying to take into account the thickness of the glass between us and the possibility that her hearing was degraded.

She thought for a second before she nodded and raised her thumb. I noticed that the man was still walking towards me, but slowly now. I was not going to stick around to find out what he wanted.

I unlocked my car, jumped in and started the engine. Before pulling my seatbelt on I accelerated backwards out of the space and off down the ramp. I zoomed down the levels as fast as I could, till I reached the barrier at ground level.

I had my ticket, but had failed to complete my payment, so halted at the barrier, wound down my window partly and pressed the *'Assistance Required'* button.

"Hello Sir. What seems to be the problem?" a crackly voice asked.

"Umm. My ticket is broken. Torn. I can't pay. Sorry," I stammered.

"Right. I will be down in a moment," he said and the intercom went silent.

The barrier looked flimsy enough, but there was a security camera aimed at my car so I was reluctant to act rashly unless I had to. I looked over both shoulders at the ramp and stairwell behind. No one was coming. Maybe I had imagined the man's interest in me. I was probably just being paranoid. The engine ticked over. My neck ached from the strain of scanning my blind spots around me, so I turned back to face the front and pulled my seatbelt across my waist. Click.

Some movement in my rear-view mirror caught my attention. A chubby man in grubby overalls with keys jangling from his belt strolled down the ramp. I leaned out of the window.

"Are you here to help me?" I asked.

"Yes sir. Let's see your ticket please," he asked.

He had the same voice as the person on the intercom, which reassured me. I reached across to the passenger seat and picked up my ticket. I tore it and waited for the garage attendant to reach the window before handing it to him.

"Sorry. I don't know how it happened," I said.

Suddenly I noticed the other man as he walked from the stairwell. He looked sinister with sunglasses on.

"Here's twenty pounds," I said and offered the attendant the money. "Please open the barrier."

"I have to get your change first," he said as he took the money.

"No need. Just open the barrier now please."

"Okay, sir. Thank you," he said, while he jangled his keys.

The ominous looking man walked closer. The attendant found a small key and unlocked the side cover on the barrier and pressed a button. The barrier raised quickly. I turned and saw the man stop where he was, about five metres short of the car.

"Stop right there," he yelled, as he pulled something metallic from his inner breast jacket pocket. It was a gun. Bloody hell. He raised it quickly, levelling it at me. I saw him squeeze the trigger and heard a distant click, but nothing happened. He sneered and started running towards me while also adjusting the gun.

I pushed the gearstick into first and pressed my right foot to the floor as I squeezed the steering wheel so hard that my knuckles turned white. I didn't want to stay around to find out what it felt like to get shot. I left a trail of smoke as the tyres screamed and the car flew up the car park exit ramp into the sunshine.

Twelve

I couldn't be certain that I hadn't been followed. I needed to do some more evasive driving, which in essence meant driving round the houses again, keeping a close eye on my rear-view mirror for any double sightings of vehicles.

As I turned onto the south circular I started panicking that because I'd left the car unattended for so long the criminals may have found it and installed a global positioning tracking system, or maybe a surveillance team had been changing vehicles as they followed, making it impossible to detect any double sightings. Tiredness and hunger had caused me to chase shadows.

I needed sugar, as the world became blurred again. It was a scary feeling to have while driving, so concentrating really hard I managed to pull into a fast food restaurant. I stopped opposite the building's entrance so I could keep an eye on the vehicle from inside.

I slumped into a window seat with a burger and chips, where I could also see the front door. Old habits, which served me well given the situation. The burger in my hands shook as I raised it to my mouth.

I called Stu's mobile as I gazed out of the window. Jennifer and I had been reluctant to give a seven year old a mobile, but it was difficult to deny him, given all his friends had one and it was useful if we were running late to pick him up.

"Hi," Stu said. There was the noise of other children laughing and shouting in the background.

"Stu?"

"Yep."

"It's me, Dad. How are you?"

"Good thanks."

"Where are you? It's very noisy," I said.

"School. It's the end of the day. Mum's picking me up in ten minutes," he said. I shuddered with fear.

"I told your Mum it isn't safe... Don't worry. I'll call her. Stay with the teacher Stu. I love you," I said and closed the phone. I rang Jennifer straight away.

"What's going on Jennifer? I told you it's not safe for Stu to be at school right now."

"Don't be so juvenile. You can't order us around anymore. Stu's perfectly safe."

"How do you know?"

"He's fine. Stop calling me with your stupid stories," she said.

"Look, I found a dead body the other day and now the killers are after me. I'm on the run from them. Please just take Stu to your Mum's house," I blurted.

"No.... Greg said it's safe."

I sighed loudly.

"He said you were overreacting. He said nothing's going to happen to me or Stu. Leave us alone, Joe."

She hung up. I was left wondering why Greg would put Jennifer and Stu in danger. What the hell was going on? I needed to speak with Stu in person. I waved at the stewardess from across the restaurant and did the international signal for the bill. She walked over and handed it to me on a platter. I put my credit card down, but something was bothering me. The waitress walked back with a card machine and put my card in the slot.

"Everything okay for you today? Please enter your pin," she said.

"Yes thanks," I replied, while punching in the numbers.

Then I froze as I'd figured it out: my credit cards could be traced. If the criminals were good enough to forge passports then they might also have the technology or contacts to locate me from credit card transactions. Damn. I needed to stop using them. It was too late though as the waitress smiled at me.

"There you go. Have a good day," she said as she handed my card back with a receipt.

I needed to move. As I left the restaurant I noticed a cash point by the door. I might as well take advantage of the service, since my card may have already been traced.

I had four credit cards and one current account card on my person. One after another I withdrew the maximum amount possible from each account. My wallet was bulging after the first three hundred pounds, so I stuffed money inside my jacket pockets. A small queue of people formed behind me as I finished with the last card. Someone behind laughed.

"You robbing the place? Leave some money for us," a man joked as I turned to walk away.

I started the car and headed home, which I knew was a bad idea but I had to see Stu one last time before I did what I had to do. I had no intention of simply driving up to the front door though. I knew my neighbourhood and felt confident I could get in and out of the house without detection from anybody who may have been waiting for me. At the bottom of my back garden there was another garden, which belonged to a house in a cul-de-sac on the opposite side of the block. I drove cautiously into the cul-de-sac and parked up to wait.

I knew Stu would be in his room watching television by himself in the early evening, while Jennifer watched her favourite soap on television downstairs. I called Stu on his mobile.

"Dad?" Stu answered.

"Hi Stu. Yes it's me. Are you in your room by yourself?" I asked.

"Yes, Dad."

"I need to meet you now. I'm going to climb up to your room and see you. Is Mum downstairs?" I asked.

"Yes, with a friend."

"Don't tell them I'm coming. This will be a secret meeting between us. Understand?" I said.

I said bye and made my way to the side gate of the house I knew backed onto my garden. I half jumped and half fell over the fence into a pile of mulch. Some lights were on in the house, but I ran down the length of their back garden and quietly performed the same 'acrobatics' again, this time falling onto my lawn with a thump. Not pretty, but I'd got there.

I brushed off the dirt on my coat and picked up some money that had fallen out. The last thing I wanted to do was lose money on my own lawn. Stu leaned out of his window and waved. His room was on the right of the house on the first floor. Lights were on in the sitting room of the ground floor, with the silhouettes of two people on the settee. They had their backs to the window, watching television. I even recognised the TV characters of Jennifer's favourite soap playing out some awful scene through the net curtains. I had twenty minutes or so before it finished. Perfect. It was dusk, so was happy to run the length of the garden.

There was a water-butt at the corner of the house, below the drainpipe, which I'd fixed only a year before. I hopped onto it and looked up to Stu's window. The pipe led up to the roof guttering above. Stu stared down at me, sniggering as I started my ascent. It had been a while since I'd climbed anything. I knew my method was far from elegant or quick, but when I reached his window ledge, I was glad to know I still had it in me. Stu offered his hand, but I was afraid to take it, as I needed to grip something solid to hoist myself through the window. Instead, I grabbed the brickwork and pulled. My middle-aged body fell to the floor in exhaustion.

"What's going on, Dad?" he asked.

"Well, Stu, I need to talk with you." I said out of breath. "I've been busy on a case recently."

"To find Dipa?" Stu asked.

"Yes." I said, pleased that he'd remembered.

"There've been some problems. There are some bad men after me and I need to get away from them," I listened to myself and realised Stu had no idea what I was babbling on about. I just wanted to see him. "How's school going?" I asked.

"It's okay. I miss Dipa."

"I'm sorry, Stu."

"Did her parents make her disappear?" he asked.

"What do you mean?"

"Dipa told me that her parents broke her arm," he mumbled.

I heard some distant movement from downstairs and then the signature creaks from our staircase; someone was coming. I checked my watch; it was too early for Stu's bedtime and Jennifer's programme should still be on. I had nowhere to hide in his small room.

"Stu, I've got to go."

I took a deep breath, holding back the hurt in the pit of my stomach. I didn't want to leave him. I crossed to the open window and began to climb out. There was a knock on the door.

"Do you want some hot chocolate Stu? I'm making some," asked Jennifer, through the door.

I lowered my body down and reached to the side, to grip my legs around the drainpipe.

"When will I see you again?" Stu whispered, as he leaned out of the window.

I didn't want to lie to him, but I couldn't tell him the truth either.

"Stu? Can I come in?" Jennifer called.

"Bye Stu. I love you."

Thirteen

I drove to yet another hotel that evening. My hotel chain loyalty account would've looked very healthy from all of the recent visits, if I'd used it, but I hadn't because it could have been used to locate me. I ate some dinner at a nearby Indian restaurant, paying with cash before collapsing onto another bed in another hotel and stared at the ceiling, with the light still on. I convinced myself that I needed the element of surprise if I were to catch the criminals responsible.

My mind wandered and I remembered the waste basket in the farmhouse. I had yet to look at the contents. Excitedly, I found the bag and emptied it onto the outer blanket of my bed. It formed a pile of tangled strips of photographic paper. I wondered whether the pieces could be reassembled, like solving a puzzle so began to fit them together.

Initially, I separated the white paper from the various coloured pieces of photographs. Half an hour quickly passed and I had formed six passport photographs of young men and women. They all looked miserable, with one even crying.

I pulled the remaining parts together and was shocked to find it formed a picture of Dipa. She stared out at me with tired red eyes. I finally had evidence that she had been imprisoned by those criminals at the farm. After days of concentrating on myself, I realised that I was the lucky one; at least I still had my freedom and my life. Dipa may have lost both. I rediscovered my hunger to solve this case and find that little girl.

I wondered how many of these seven people had newly forged passports and how many ended their days in a white sheet like the poor soul I'd found. Each of the pictures on my bed had something wrong, either the subject's eyes were shut, they weren't facing straight ahead, or the photograph was blurred. Dipa's photograph had a mark in the top right corner. I knew there were strict rules about what photograph could be accepted for use in a passport, so I came to the conclusion that they must have all been thrown away because they simply didn't make the grade.

I pulled out the five passports I'd also taken from the farmhouse and matched two of the seven people from the reclaimed pictures on my bed. I studied one of the passports under the desk lamp. It belonged to a Ralph Klein and was of a good quality. It was difficult to tell if it was a forgery or not, which gave me an idea.

I shuffled through the other passports and found the passport without a picture. The date of birth was only two years younger than me and it belonged to a male called Gavin Whittaker. In a moment of madness I decided I could make the passport my own. If I was going to find these criminals, then I needed to follow the people covertly and I could think of no better way than under an alias passport.

At first I scared myself with the thought of pretending to be someone else. It was illegal, but everything I needed was in hand and I was also excited by the prospect: I could be like a spy during the Cold War, fleeing a Soviet Bloc country while disguised as a fictitious character.

My brain whirred into action. I needed a scalpel, glue and a sheet of sticky-back cellophane, but first I needed a passport photo of myself. It was 9:00pm. I wouldn't have been able to sleep if I'd waited until the following morning, so was galvanized to throw on a coat and find a supermarket that was still open.

By 10:30pm I'd returned to my room with all the items, including four passport photos still sticky to the touch. Under the glare of the desk lamp, I carefully cut out a picture with an art scalpel, before cutting the cellophane to the size of the passport back page. With the photograph placed exactly in the correct location on the flattened passport page, I brought down the sticky cellophane and squashed out all of the trapped air bubbles from the middle to the edges. It stuck perfectly.

My new name was going to be Gavin Whittaker. Although I'd been a PI for many years, I had never undertaken anything quite as daring as forging a passport. The prospect of posing as someone else for an extended length of time was very exciting. I smiled at the thought of using the criminal's own tools against them.

I knew that my transformation wouldn't be complete till I'd disposed of all of my current identification, but it would appear odd if I just disappeared, particularly if the criminals suspected I might do just that. If the tables were turned and I was the hunter rather than the prey, I would certainly re-double my efforts if someone managed to get away from me. Call it professional pride or stubbornness, either way I would ensure that I found them.

I needed to somehow guarantee that the criminals would stop searching for me. The only way of doing this would be to fake my own death. If this was done carefully and the transition from my current self to Gavin Whittaker was not observed by any witnesses, then I had a good chance of making a clean getaway. However, I had some further work before that could be attempted.

I thought about the ideal location, where no one would be around. It would have to be somewhere legitimate for me to be and if I was going to 'die' then I needed to leave a body behind that looked like me, which is pretty much impossible given the modern advances in forensics. Even if I could locate a dead body, my big problem was DNA, as everyone has a unique signature and my own DNA would have been impossible to fake.

Given these problems, my body needed to disappear forever, which narrowed down where the transition from me to my reincarnated alter-ego could take place. The most obvious location was at sea, where I'd heard of bodies going missing through unexplained incidents or sinking boats.

I turned the lights off at midnight but hardly slept that night as I re-examined whether I was doing the best thing. I knew Stu would be devastated to hear about my death, but I also knew that as long as I was alive, he and Jennifer would be in danger. The criminals would surely take out their aggression on my family if they could not find me. Faking my own death also seemed to be the only way to guarantee their safety.

I contemplated the fact that I would have to cut my ties with everything I knew in my life, not just my credit cards and mobile, but even Stu. I couldn't send him an e-mail in case someone monitored his messages in an attempt to locate me. Everything would have to stop. That was the toughest part, but it had to be done.

I already knew the location I would be heading. The passports were all Maltese and the address I had noted from the farmhouse was in Malta, so this was where my investigations would resume.

It was sunny that morning, which seemed to be perfect weather to visit a beach. I wanted to recce a suitable location for my demise and had one particular beach in mind, in Brighton. After a liquid breakfast consisting of a strong sugary coffee, which would have been strongly disapproved of by my diabetes doctor, I set off. I'd visited Brighton beach as a child with my parents and had fond memories of the sunshine, skimming stones over the waves and playing on the slot machines by the pier. I had even taken Jennifer on occasion and introduced her to the quirky side streets and picturesque views.

I soaked my lungs in the sea air as I strolled along the rugged concrete path between the beach and road. The seagulls quarrelled noisily over a dropped ice-cream cone and crusts from a sandwich. I knew I didn't have enough money to live on for any length of time overseas. I thought about selling the car, but knew it would look suspicious to the police and the criminals if I sold my car just before a fatal accident. To avoid jeopardizing my discovery I pushed the temptation of this easy cash injection to the back of my mind.

While I was reacquainting myself with the sights of Brighton, I came across an internet cafe and paid a woman at the counter one pound for thirty minutes internet surfing. Through the window I made out some hardened locals who were out on their long boards doing the real thing.

I sent Stu a message for the last time, to wish him well at school. Of course I didn't mention anything of my plan, so kept my message as light hearted as I could muster. I researched how to get myself to Malta, as I was unsure of the route to take from the UK for a man in my financial condition, while also avoiding the larger customs and immigration offices.

Flying from the UK to Malta would have been straightforward, if I was unconcerned about being scrutinised. The problem was that UK airports are brimming with security so I doubted I would've got onto any plane. Although I had faith in the quality of my passport, I didn't want to push my luck by handing it to a seasoned customs official who examines thousands on a daily basis. Flying was also too expensive, so I preferred to take the slower but safer route out of the UK, leaving from a smaller port by boat, as there would be fewer people transiting and the officials maybe less stringent with passport checks. It was a gamble whichever route I took though.

Next I had to decide how to fake my death. I could either be swimming in the sea and drown, or hire a boat and fall overboard. In either scenario the important thing was to ensure that there was good reason to believe that my body was never detected. I preferred the idea of hiring a boat, as someone would raise the alarm when their boat was not returned, so my disappearance would be noticed and reported. This was of course what I wanted, so that eventually everyone would conclude that I was dead. I knew that UK law stated that a person could only be declared legally dead after seven years of being listed as missing.

I searched the internet for a 'boat hire in Brighton' and found somewhere close by. I logged off and walked out of the shop with a plan, with only some of the details yet to be set.

A short walk along the coast from the beach, I found the small beachfront boat repair shop that was advertised online as a place to also hire boats. An old man was diligently rolling black paint onto the raised hull of a large vessel with an extended roller. The hull was suspended above the gently sloping concrete track by a steel frame structure. The vessel was positioned halfway between a covered workshop at the top of the slope and the sea at the bottom. The man wore black jogging bottoms, a red puffer jacket and green trainers with flecks of black paint on them. He was a balding fellow with leathery skin, probably from years of exposure to the elements. I headed towards him on the stones, which crackled beneath my feet.

"Hello there," he said, still engrossed in his work.

"Hello. Do you have a boat I can hire?" I asked.

"What sort of boat, son?" he said, still rolling on the paint.

"Something small to take out for a day, to do some fishing," I said.

"Fishing, eh?" he put the paint roller down and stepped out from under the hull. "Well I've a rowing boat. There's plenty of Mackerel just offshore. Caught four myself just last week."

"Great. Thanks." I said "Can I come back tomorrow to hire it?"

"Whenever you want. I'm always 'ere. I just need a deposit before you take 'er out. Have a good 'un," he said and picked up his roller again.

"Great. Thanks so much. I'll be back tomorrow," I said.

The plan was materialising. I felt nervous at the thought that I could actually do it. I looked out at sea and paused for thought before I walked back across the stones and picked a speckled smooth flat stone from the billions strewn across the beach. I played with its cold smoothness between my fingers and walked to the water's edge. I leaned forward slightly and flicked my wrist, as I threw it over the crest of the nearest wave. I playfully decided that if the stone bounced more than three times then I would go ahead with my plan.

It span out and grazed the water's surface before bouncing one, two, three, four, five, maybe six times and then sunk. It was stupid, I know, but I needed something to reassure me, to cement the decision in my mind. I had the realisation that I would actually be faking my own death tomorrow.

Fourteen

I ate some freshly deep-fried cod and chips the traditional way, from yesterday's newspaper, while sitting on a bench overlooking the sea. The three surfers who had dominated the waterfront since my arrival eventually paddled back to land as the sky overhead filled with cloud.

I returned to my old rust bucket of a vehicle as large raindrops began to fall. A casual look through the windows showed anyone who cared to look that I'd been living in there a while, with a sprinkling of food packaging, kit, clothes and other clutter across all seats. It had always been unkempt, but by that time my car was messier than Stu's most extravagant hand painting he had made when he was three.

I made a list of essentials that I needed to take with me when my new life started. Most important were clothes, insulin supplies, some cereal bars, my newly personalised passport and money. I included the fairly expensive watch on my wrist, which could be sold if, or when, I ran out of money. Everything else was a luxury because I simply didn't have the space to take much else with me.

I packed all essentials into one plastic bag. In a separate plastic bag a packed a towel, so my clothes would remain dry while I dried. The bags needed to be placed somewhere where they would not be disturbed, but close enough to the seafront where I could find them quickly after getting out of the water. I didn't want to be left exposed in the cold for long. Finding the ideal location was the next task of the day.

The rain pattered on the car roof as I drove along the small coastal roads a mile or so till, through the trees, I spotted a rocky outcrop in a secluded bay. It was the perfect place to come ashore without detection as it was far enough from the beaches and coastal towns, with no buildings around.

I found my hands trembling nervously as I parked up on the side of the road. With my hazard lights on and bags in hand I made my way over some large boulders at the roads edge and through the trees to the waterline. I noted the high tide mark, where lumps of seaweed concentrated along the beach and found a perfect location for my plastic bags above this line, behind a large boulder.

It occurred to me that the coastline looked much the same in all directions. I ran back to the car and grabbed the reflective hazard triangle, the sort you put on the road following a breakdown in the road, along with some red cord and scissors. I tied the triangle tightly to a tree near the boulder with the cord, which made a great landmark that could easily be seen from the sea. It would act as my personal lighthouse.

I didn't know what Maltese food was like, but I doubted Malta appreciated the English classics, so that evening I ate one of my all time favourites for what was to be my last supper in my own name; juicy steak and ale pie with crisp, thick cut chips, peas and gravy. Delicious.

That night I felt like a restless child waiting for Christmas Eve to end, but also tinged with hesitation. I didn't give a damn about Jennifer would feel, as she had made it perfectly clear that she didn't give a damn, but Stu could be deeply affected by the death of his father. I was comforted by the thought that my transformation wasn't forever. I planned to return as soon as possible, once the criminals were captured and Dipa was found.

The following morning I told myself that there were no further dress rehearsals; today was D-day. Upon my return to Brighton beach car park, I paid for four hours parking and put the ticket in the car. During the final search of the car I came across my pair of binoculars and a waterproof torch in the boot, which were both useful additions to my kit. I tapped the roof of the car in a gesture that acknowledged that I may not see the old banger ever again. We'd been through many adventures together and I would miss her.

Before pushing off in a boat, I had one last shopping spree to complete. Since I was meant to be fishing, I had to make the story believable and purchase a fishing rod, from a local beachfront shop. I purchased a short rod that extended with a float, a bucket and some squid to use as bait, as I knew Mackerel were partial to this. I paid by credit card deliberately, as I planned to be long gone by the time anyone worked out the transaction was in Brighton. The last time I'd been fishing was a few months earlier. My dad had introduced me to the sport when I was teenager and had taken to it regularly from then as a great stress relief.

I headed back to my fisherman friend, who was still where I had left him, painting the hull of the same vessel, but this time he was leaning perilously over the edge of the deck some height above the concrete ramp below. He had a brush in hand and was touching up the wooden trim on the port side.

"Good morning," I called gently, not wanting to scare him and be responsible for him falling.

"Mornin'. Here for the rowing boat, are we?" he asked as he looked at me from head to toe.

"Yes please. Do you take credit card for the deposit?"

"Yes. That'll be fine. Come with me to the office," he said, putting the brush in the tin and wiping his hands on a rag cloth.

He climbed down the steps at the stern of the boat onto the concrete slope. We walked down the gradient and between two tall sliding wooden doors, into a large workshop. I noticed on our walk that the fisherman had a limp, but he looked the sort of man not to complain about it. There were two other smaller boats in the back of the building next to the winch that was holding the vast weight of the vessel he had been painting on the beachfront.

We walked into a side room, where the man sat at a desk with a credit card machine. I handed over my plastic and he swiped it. I didn't even ask how much it would be or whether I would get the money back afterwards. I simply didn't care and he forgot to tell me.

"There we go," he said, "here is the receipt." He handed me a slip of paper which I pushed into a pocket. "The boat is at the back. I'll help you get it to the water line."

"Thank you."

I placed my fishing equipment into the boat, next to the oars. We each held a side of the rowing boat and shuffled it down the ramp. We placed the small boat into the water. My inexperience showed as I got my shoes, socks and trousers wet up to my knee while the fisherman had oversize wellington boots on and stayed dry.

"When will you be back?" he asked. "I close at four."

"Probably after lunch," I lied.

He turned and headed back up the slope. I placed a few handfuls of the large rocks at the edge of the water into the boat, as I would need them later. I hopped in and made the boat sway violently, but I avoided the embarrassment of rolling overboard by sitting quickly. The boat drifted away from the shore as I manoeuvred the ores into their rowlocks. With this completed, I turned the boat slowly to face the beach and pulled away to set me free from the land.

The shore appeared to float further and further away. The rhythmical sound of the waves hitting the rocky beach faded till all I could hear was the creaking of the boat and soft lapping of water on the sides. I felt the wind whistle through my hair. At about a hundred metres offshore I could no longer see the bottom of the sea.

With some splashing and clanking, I turned the boat and altered my course to row parallel to the coast in the direction of my bay. I became hot and sweaty after what must have been half an hour of sustained effort. I stopped, through my binoculars I could see that I was making good progress, but judged I was only about halfway to my destination.

I needed to rest a while before continuing, so reached into my bag of tricks. I pulled out a gleaming expandable fishing rod and attached some bait to the hock. I cast the bait as far towards the dark blue horizon as my tired arms would allow. It had been years since I'd last fished in the sea. I held the rod and stared at the distant bobbing float. After awhile I simply and very deliberately dropped the rod overboard. It and then the float submerged. It was time to go to work.

I picked up the ores and pulled once more. It felt like the fibres in my arm muscles were ripping as I strained to drag the boat through the water. I daydreamed that I had hired an extravagantly large and comfortable speed boat with leather seats and a sundeck. If I'd hired such a thing of beauty, I would have put the hire costs onto Jennifer's credit card. That would have ruined her day. I chuckled freely at the fantasy.

My poor quality rowing and the currents slowed my journey, but after a lot of luck, I was only about a kilometre from shore and opposite the red reflective triangle, which I could make out through the binoculars quite clearly, amongst the green trees. It was 3:00pm. I had to move quickly to get to shore before the light faded. The sun was already low in the partially cloudy sky.

I glanced around one last time to check for fishing boats or surfers. I was alone. I tested the temperature of the water with a finger. It was freezing, but I convinced myself that I wasn't going to be in for long. I took all my clothes off apart from my boxers. I systematically tied each item of clothing around a rock and checked to ensure that it wouldn't come free, as my clothes had to sink to the bottom and never be found. My existence needed to appear to end in the murky water below. The rocky parcels were dropped overboard. My trousers, t-shirt, coat, each shoe and sock and jumper were all disposed of.

I left my wallet and car keys in the boat with the bucket of bait, where they were likely to be found, in time. Holding only my torch and binoculars, I lowered myself into the water quickly and instinctively gasped for air. I shuddered at the cold and swam hard towards land.

The cold sapped my ability to think and once I was out of breath, my arms flailed awkwardly as I tried to keep my head above the water. A large wave pushed me to the side and filled my left ear with seawater. I shook my head and swam again.

I tried to regain some strength and so treaded water for a while, looking around and down. I could see nothing but perfect blackness below me. I felt like I was disappearing into the ocean. My inner demons tortured me with thoughts of monsters in the ocean surging towards my legs and reaching out to drag me to the deep.

I saw the light of a ship on the horizon. It was probably the ferry from Newhaven to Dieppe that I'd planned to take me far away to my new life. Instead, I was stuck in a self-imposed hell. Every minute that ticked by, the sun sank lower. I knew with certainty that darkness meant death. I began to panic.

My arms were getting heavier and breathing faster. The surging water pressed against my tiring torso, expelling any fight I had to stay alive. I swam as fast as I could towards shore, but barely made any progress. The tides were pulling me out to sea, which was becoming more violent.

Large waves subsumed me with their white tips and steep sides. I screamed pathetically and knew no one could hear. I felt completely sorry for myself and so cold. I had to keep moving to stay alive. I dropped my binoculars as they were useless to me and tried swimming again.

In the dusk, I misjudged the height of an approaching wave which rolled over my head. I choked on the salty water and pulled myself high above the ensuing spray to take a lungful of air, to partially recover. Another wave hit me. Nothing could help me. I was choking and cold. My arms and legs felt so heavy and numb.

I longed for the warmth of a tropical island. I wondered what Stu would look like when he was older, what would he end up doing. I gave up. My lungs burned. I couldn't keep fighting or I didn't want to keep fighting. Either way, I closed my eyes as my head sunk beneath the waves. I went down and down but never felt the bottom.

Fifteen

There should be no pain after death. I knew from the cold and throbbing at the back of my head that I was still alive. In those hazy moments before I lost consciousness I remembered considering the existence of God. I must have been in a bad way given I'd been a steadfast atheist up until that point.

I was resting on some rocks, but stayed there for a moment, to regain some perspective and assess what was wrong with me. Nothing hurt that badly. I shivered violently and pushed myself to my feet. I must have been near shore when I passed out. It was dark and I was freezing. By some stroke of luck I had the torch, which was still tied to my wrist.

I looked up and down the coast, wondering which way to go. I recognised a tall building in the distance and that I must have been in the right general area to find my package of clothes and money. I flicked on the torch and began to walk. I kept moving forward across the rocks, pebbles and sometimes boulders, towards some distant trees.

I fanned the torch ahead of me, sweeping the tree line. About a hundred metres ahead the beam reflected off something shiny and red. It could only have been my reflective warning triangle. Encouraged, I walked faster until I reached my precious packages. I rustled the plastic bag, but my numb fingers made me clumsy. I eventually was able to rip it open with my teeth, to recover my towel. I dried myself as best as I could. I had sand stuck to my side and earth and leaves on my feet, but brushed this all off before opening the next bag.

I stripped naked in the darkness, while the wind blew past. I redressed quickly and felt warmer and stronger. I ate my supplies, but still felt hungry and thirsty. Not packing water into my bags had been an obvious oversight. I walked up the slope through the trees, to the country road I'd driven along earlier that day as Joe Patterson. I reminded myself aloud that my name was now Gavin Whittaker. My reincarnation had been far more painful than I'd hoped, but I made it.

The ferry I'd planned to take had long since departed. I walked along the edge of the deserted and unlit road to the bus stop that I had discovered during my trawl of transportation options on the internet. The last bus was at 10:00pm. I had missed it by twenty minutes. Disheartened and tired, I decided to wait under the cover of the bus shelter till the next one arrived, which according to the timetable was due at 06:35am the following day.

It started raining shortly after. The rain first tapped on the roof and then hammered loudly. The leaves on a stinging nettle just outside were beaten to the ground by the force of the torrent. A small stream formed and ran down the edge of the road. I took the opportunity of cupping my hands outside my shelter to collect rain water to drink.

I made myself as comfortable as possible, lying on my back on the wooden bench inside the well maintained shelter. I imagined eating succulent spaghetti bolognaise, followed by chocolate cake with ice-cream and chocolate sauce. I did a lot of serious thinking that night too. As I got more and more tired, I tortured myself with thoughts of Jennifer, Stu and Greg living together as a happy family. I had to open my eyes and force myself to wake up to stop the stupid thoughts rattling around my head.

Finally during a period of dozing, I heard the low rumblings of the first bus of the morning, which stopped feet from my tired body. The bus driver opened the automatic door and tilted his head in my direction.

"Rough night?" he chirped, all to cheerfully.

I stretched and pushed myself up to the vertical position.

"Yep. Do you go to Newhaven?"

"Sure do. That's two pound sixty please, sir," he replied.

I paid the fare and settled into a seat in the middle of the empty bus, leaning against the window. I was thankful for the relative warmth and comfort of the bus after so long on a bench. The rocking of the bus as it swayed forward soon put me to sleep. What seemed like only a moment later, the driver woke me with a series of loud shouts.

"This is Newhaven Port," the bus driver bellowed repeatedly, for my benefit.

There were several old aged pensioners with purple rinses now on the bus with me, who were as startled as me by the driver's calls. Wearily I stepped off the bus to see the ferry terminal ahead. I had to have my wits about me, as I mentally prepared to have my alias tested by the UK border guards. I took out my new passport and reminded myself of my date and place of birth, before noticing some CCTV cameras ahead. I put my hood up and walked past them to reach the entrance of the ferry terminal.

I bought a ticket to Dieppe, as I had planned. Before I could get to the passenger waiting area, I had to pass through the customs and immigration desk. There were two young and enthusiastic looking officers on duty that morning.

I walked to the nearest desk with my head held high and tried to move my arms freely by my side, to hide my growing sense of trepidation. I presented my passport with a smile, while I made a throwaway comment about the weather. The Customs officer opened the passport and examined it. He rubbed the page and looked carefully.

It occurred to me at that moment that I needed to do something extraordinary. Off-the-cuff and without any great consideration I quietly hummed 'Bob the Builder'. It was a strange choice, but the first thing that came into my head. The Customs official glanced at me and shuffled uncomfortably, before he continued with his duties. I repeated my eccentric distraction.

"Umm. What is your purpose of travel today sir?" he asked.

I stopped humming.

"I'm going for the day to France, to look around and do a bit of shopping," I said.

He carefully examined my face and looked down at my document again.

"Sorry. It's a catchy tune. I can't get it out my head," I said. "Stupid really."

He closed my passport, with a resigned look on his face.

"Enjoy your day," I said and walked past.

I waited in the already bulging waiting room, which seemed to be full of Frenchmen. I had studied French at school, but struggled terribly. I just didn't have the patience to learn it. I had visited Biarritz as a school exchange student, where I lived for a week with a very welcoming French family. My abiding memory was the amazing food that the mother served every evening. I ate like a king while I was there.

I knew as I overheard the French conversations in that waiting room, that it would feel more awkward than normal to not be able to understand the locals. The only consolation was that I was only travelling through and it was another opportunity to have some mouth-watering food.

Once the boat was ready to receive us, we were ushered onboard. Confident that I didn't suffer from seasickness, I sat in the top deck away from the smelly toilets. As the boat's horn blasted out on departure, I felt a great sense of achievement.

I pick up the glass on the table to take a sip of water. I don't know how long I have been talking, but my throat is raw. It's taking forever, but I do not want to skip over any detail that may prove to be important. I want to be as truthful as possible to the police.

"So, Joe, it seems you are also guilty of fraud, as well as the drug and people smuggling crimes," Inspector Bosco finally says.

"What?" I say.

"Life insurance fraud," he says sharply.

"No. I faked my death to escape from the maniacs trying to kill me. I never meant to steal anything," I say.

"So, why did you sign up for an extensive life insurance policy, just a few weeks before you disappeared?"

"That's a coincidence. I never knew at the time..." I insist.

"Right, a coincidence then," he repeats and lets it hang in the air.

"I never meant to. I forgot all about the insurance once those killers came after me," I insist.

"You've been living in Malta for about a month now, and at no time did you remember to call the insurance company to explain the error? All you had to do was make one phone call to cancel it," the policeman says.

"But if I'd called, then I would let them know that I was still alive and then my family would have been put in danger."

"I find that very convenient... Of course, any money received unlawfully by your son will have to be returned and the insurance company may wish to press charges too."

"Yep, of course," I say reluctantly.

"I can't believe you still don't understand," I say, losing my patience, "I had other priorities when I fled the country, like staying alive! I didn't give a damn about the insurance money. I wanted to find and stop those killers."

"Why didn't you call the police for help?" he asks.

"I don't trust the police."

"Because of what happened to your brother, right?" he guesses.

I remain silent.

"So you think you're above the law?"

"Look, I'm no hero and I'm certainly not above the law. I'm a private investigator."

"I see. So you aren't working in the drugs cartel?" the Inspector asks.

"Absolutely not. The bastards tried to kill me," I say angrily.

"So as a private investigator, do you regularly follow people covertly and snoop on their private lives?"

"That's an element of the job, yes."

"Is it fair to say that you've honed your skills to deceive people while being a private investigator?"

"Deceive people? I don't do that."

"When you meet people you're spying on, you pretend to be someone else, don't you?"

"Sometimes, but only when I have to."

"So given that you lie to people for a living, how can I trust anything you say, Joe?"

I feel exacerbated and sigh loudly as I look down at the table. He had a point though.

"One more question before you continue your story, do you know Nicodermus Antonelli?"

"Absolutely not. I've never heard of him," I lie to his face.

The truth is that I had met Nicodemus, in a luxurious Maltese office hidden beneath the scorched earth. I also know why the police are so keen to find him, because he is a drug lord, responsible for coordinating a cartel that stretches across Europe that supplies and manipulates the class A drug markets. The problem I have is that I promised him that I would never reveal his identity and he blackmailed me to keep this promise, so I've got no option but to lie to the police.

Sixteen

It took just three days to reach Malta. I stuck to public transport that didn't have to be pre-booked, mostly trains, to keep a low profile. I travelled via Dieppe to Paris, on to Beaune and crossed the border into Italy at Mont Blanc, down the coast to Villa San Giovanni, via Florence. From there I caught a ferry to Messina and onto Catania, before taking another ferryboat to the Maltese capital, Valletta. I sailed into Valletta sitting on the uncovered decking, warming my bones in the sunshine and squinting at the white cliffs of the surrounding coast. It's a beautiful country, like something I could only dream of. Sheer perfection.

It had been an intense time for me, with non-stop travel because I was keen to get to Malta as soon as possible of my 'demise', in case my photo was released to any border agencies. I needed to remain below the radar, to maintain the element of surprise from my would be assassins.

Once on the island, I simply wanted to rest in a quiet hotel, but there was work to do. I had no greatly conceived master plan, just the Maltese address that I'd found at the farmhouse in Shere, but first I needed somewhere as a base.

I walked into Valletta, on the uneven cobbled stoned pavements, till I found a small hotel off a side street called 'Hotel Central'. It was a rustic building with a helpful hotel manager who, in broken English, agreed that I could pay for a room on a daily basis and stay as long as I needed.

My room was a generous size, with a Juliet balcony overlooking a pretty town square, covered in multi-coloured pansies. After dumping my bags and taking a refreshing shower, I was in need of a large drink, to help unwind. I headed out onto the narrow streets and strolled around the block to a bar, called 'The Zoltan', which was open, but virtually deserted. I pulled up a stool and joined the barman to be sociable. He was an old man, maybe in his seventies.

"Hello. Can I get a beer please?" I asked.

"What brings you to town?" he said, as he poured a locally brewed draft and placed it on a beer mat in front of me.

"Business, mainly. I've not visited Malta before and never realised how peaceful it is," I said in an attempt to take the focus of the conversation away from myself, as I hated lying to people.

"What business are you in?" he persisted.

"Fishing," I said, thankful that I'd prepared a basic cover story.

"Of course. You look like a fisherman," he said and nodded. "It hasn't always been so peaceful here you know," he continued, while I sipped my cold beer. "Mile for mile, Malta was the most bombed place on Earth in the 1940s."

"Really? Why?" I asked eager to learn more.

"The Germans thought Malta was a vital stepping stone to North Africa. They bombed the hell out of us! The only place we could go to escape from the bombs was underground. The sewers were converted into public bunkers. My sister and I lived out most of the war in those smelly tunnels."

I looked at the barman's old face more closely and saw the countless wrinkles. He'd clearly lived a tough life.

"That's horrible," I said, trying to imagine the stench.

"Of course, the military and officials had their own specially built tunnel networks, cut deep into the yellow limestone. Lucky buggers. The hardest thing wasn't the accommodation or the bombing runs, but the lack of food. It drove people crazy."

He picked up some used glasses from the counter and placed them in the sink behind the bar.

"It was June 1942 when the island reached starvation point. There wasn't even enough wood to light the fires to cook bread. We had nothing, so had to eat insects to stay alive. They crunched between our teeth and filled our mouths with a foul puss. Not nice."

"Wow," is all I could muster, as I shook my head in disgust.

I gulped down the remainder of my beer. Despite the bumbling barman, I stuck around for couple more hours for a few more beers and war stories, before I reached the point where I couldn't stomach any more.

"I've got to go," I said, interrupting him again. "How much do I owe you?"

"Fifteen Euros, or you could bring me some fish next time you visit," he joked.

I grimaced as he reminded me of my lie. I felt a drunken pang of guilt as I handed over the money with a generous tip.

I woke the following morning with a banging headache, which was no doubt due to the brutal combination of a verbal barrage upon my ears and a copious quantity of local beers. That barman could talk for Malta!

Instead of staying in bed, as I usually did when hung-over, I took advantage of my new life-style and headed to the beach, a short stagger away. It was another sunny day in paradise. On the pavement nearest to the beach there was a British red post-box, which looked out of place. It was reassuring to see the island remembered its British colony ties.

The sea was crystal clear and shimmered gloriously. The water surged towards the beach before running out of steam and retreating again. The beach was small and positioned between two outcrops of rocks. Surprisingly, no one else was around. I took my shoes off and planted my feet into the warm soft white sand. It was bliss and exactly as I'd imagined. I wriggled my toes and smiled with delight as I headed to the shade of a palm tree to lie down and rest my thumping head.

I looked up and saw the sunlight flutter between the gently rustling branches of the tree. I must have nodded back to sleep listening to the lapping waves, as I awoke to find the shadow of the tree had crawled away and the sunlight was warming my face. There was a sweet chorus of birds singing overhead and a plethora of sunbathers filled the beach.

My head still felt slightly foggy, but I pulled my overweight body up from the sand. I decided it was time to focus on finding the Maltese address that had been written on the note in the farmhouse. I had wasted enough time.

After using a local internet cafe to locate the exact whereabouts of the address, I took a local bus through the countryside to a town called Sliema. Within two hours, I was walking along the adjacent street and saw a three storey smartly presented white stone clad building. Bingo. I recognised this building from the street view on the internet. I approached the detached building from the left, or B-side.

The UK police and fire services use the A-B-C-D communication system for identifying the sides of buildings. I also favoured this system in my line of work, which was particularly helpful when working in a surveillance team and trying to explain over a radio to a team member which entrance to a building a mark had entered. By convention, the A-side is the front facing the street, then moving clockwise around the side of the structure, B is to the left, the C-side is at the rear and D-side is on the right.

The exterior B-side door was likely a storage cupboard that held the rubbish bins, judging by the crisp packet that was trapped under the poorly fitted door and the other giveaway was that it didn't have a lock. The rubbish bins were possibly worth further investigation at a future occasion, when there were fewer prying eyes. I could tell a lot about who lived at a property from their rubbish.

The A and B-sides of the building had pavement just outside. I walked past the front at a slow pace, taking in all the details I could without obviously staring. The sash ground floor windows appeared to be double glazed and locked. Annoyingly, the net curtains gave zero visibility within. There was a grand and wide oak front door set at street level with a large brass knocker and a brass letter box opening in the middle of the door. I noted the two locks.

The C and D-sides of the building were fenced off as a private garden. It was unclear whether the building was an executive office or large residence. I stopped at a newsagent just down the street and while browsing a magazine, turned and looked back at the rest of the road.

At this point I noticed a restaurant directly opposite the property. Given it was midday, I decided to take advantage of its location and see who came in or out, while I ate lunch. As I pulled open the front door to the Italian restaurant, I almost overlooked a small nondescript sign in the window which simply read *'waiter/waitress needed. Please apply within'*. A golden opportunity had presented itself.

I could think of no better way of metaphorically killing two birds with one stone, than earning money from a job that provided excellent cover to simultaneously carry out surveillance on a target address. If only I could get the job, I thought as I stepped inside.

An attractive middle aged woman, with long brunette hair tied in a bun and twinkly brown eyes showed me to a table by the window. She wore a waistcoat with gold buttons and a velvet black bow tie with a nicely ironed white shirt and sensible shoes.

I looked through the menu, which I asked to keep for the duration of my meal, to familiarise myself with the range of gastro-delights they had to offer. I ordered Penne Arrabiata, which consisted of macaroni pasta, chilli, tomato, garlic and basil, with a side order of Ciabatta Bread and a glass of house red. I injected myself with insulin, in preparation of the meal ahead.

While my food was being prepared, I mulled over the idea of working in Malta. Being a citizen of the European Union I knew I had the right to work. The more fundamental problem, however, was that I had no experience in the service industry, but how hard could it be, I thought? I just had to write orders, pour drinks and pick up plates...

I took long looks through the window at the building while I ate my delicious food. No one had entered or left the building by the time I'd settled the bill, so I asked the waitress about the advert in the window.

"I can introduce you to the manager if you want?" she suggested, with a cute smile. She was just my type.

"I'm Gavin. Do you like working here?" I asked and offered my hand.

"I'm Autumn," she said and I shook her hand delicately, " The hours are quite long, as we don't close until midnight most nights, but it's okay. I'm studying business studies at college, so need the money."

"You've got a lovely name," I said.

"Thank you." she said, blushing slightly, before moving the subject along. "do you want to speak with Peter?" she asked.

"Yes please, Autumn."

Some new customers sat down at an adjacent table and stared at Autumn in expectation.

"Sorry, I've got to go," she said. "But, I'll get Peter first," she smiled.

She disappeared through a swing door at the back. A minute later a man appeared, wearing a shirt and blue tie. He had short distinguished grey hair with complimentary bushy white eyebrows, which made him look like the personification of a wise great owl. He must have been in his sixties.

"Good afternoon sir. I'm Peppi," he said, offering his hand. "Did you like your food today?"

"Gavin," I said as I shook his hand. "Yes, I loved your food so much, that I'd like to be considered for the job you're advertising." I gestured towards the sign in the window.

"I see. Do you have any experience as a waiter?"

"Absolutely. Several years in London," I lied my face off, "where I worked in a Michelin Star restaurant in Mayfair." If I was going to lie, then why not go big, I thought.

"Wow. So what brings you here then?"

"I was tired of the rat race. Burnt out, so I moved to Malta."

"What languages do you speak?"

"Just English," I confessed, knowing I couldn't pretend otherwise.

"Well normally, I would expect my waiting staff to speak English, French and Italian, being the main languages of the island..." he said, as he looked across to Autumn, who stood by his side.

"I'm a very hard worker," I added, sensing failure. I smiled at him and he glanced at Autumn, as if for her guidance. She smiled sweetly.

"Well, it would be good to have someone with your experience." Peppi said, looking at me and offered his hand again, "can you start tomorrow night, on a trial basis?"

"Brilliant. Thank you," I beamed.

"6pm tomorrow. I've got spare uniforms, so just turn up as you are. Now, I must get back to work, so excuse me please." Peppi said and went back to the kitchen.

"Thank you Autumn. I have a feeling you helped him decide," I said and Autumn giggled coyly. Was she flirting with me? I couldn't be certain. I'd always been rubbish at interpreting signals from the opposite sex.

Seventeen

The rest of the afternoon I walked through central Valletta, which was dominated by the sophistically crafted dome of the Basilica. The ancient church can be viewed from anywhere in the city. I came across a small and quirky looking shop, which judging by the display in the window, seemed to be stocked with a variety of European treasures. Intrigued, I entered to see a wide range of consumable treats, such as Dutch cheese, Belgium beer and Turkish Delights. There were even Cuban cigars in stock, despite Cuba not being in Europe the last time I checked. Of all the items, the one that caught my eye was The Times newspaper.

Unfortunately all the merchandise was extortionately priced, but I paid the princely sum equivalent to four pounds sterling, as I missed my daily newspaper crossword so much. The newspaper was four days old, probably because it had been flown over from the UK. This didn't matter to me though. As a thank you to Autumn, I also bought a very neatly packaged box of Swiss chocolates.

I savoured the thought of indulging myself with every last snippet of British news, political scandal, sporting triumph and impending weather disaster. I wanted to reminisce about home, while basking in the warmth of the mid-morning Maltese sunshine. It was strange that being removed from the country which I considered to be home had made me far more intrigued by it than I had ever been while living there.

I resisted the temptation to read anything while inside the shop, although I couldn't help catch the front page headline that read: *'Tories raise Income Tax'*. Under normal circumstances, such a title would have driven me to another newspaper, but instead a wave of nostalgia overcame me.

I took the paper to a coffee shop on the seafront, where I patiently sat with it unopened till after my first cup of espresso had been delivered to my table. Only after a couple of sips did I finally allow myself the pleasure of pulling open the crisp pages and began reading from cover to cover.

During this moment of luxury, I came across something truly bizarre between the sheets near the back of the paper that filled me with intrigue; my obituary. The article was brief, only two paragraphs, and stated that I'd been missing for the last week and was presumed dead. I laughed out loud and duly received a leer from two customers at an adjoining table.

Apparently, my body had never been found, which was reassuring to read. It went on to state that my family was shocked by my disappearance, and that I was one of only twelve people whose body had never been recovered from the sea in the last year.

I read it over and over. It was surreal to be sat in a foreign land reading about my own death. I felt like a criminal mastermind who had evaded the law. It was very final to read about my own demise, in black and white and know that everyone truly believed it. On one hand, it was exactly what I'd planned and hoped for as I had fooled everyone into believing I had actually gone for good, but I was also disappointed that they had given up trying to find me.

I felt unloved and soon to be forgotten. The cynic in me thought Jennifer and Greg would have put up minimal resistance to the idea that I was dead. My untimely death was very convenient to them. I knew poor Stu would be heartbroken. I scrunched the newspaper as a pang of guilt cut into me.

That evening I was bored and lonely, so found myself once again walking into 'The Zoltan' bar to meet my vocal friend. The bar was once again virtually deserted, with just two couples who preferred the shadows of the back of the bar. They were no doubt pleased that the barman had someone to entertain him, leaving them to talk in peace.

The first story of the evening my barman friend told me was about a ninety-two-year-old called Giuseppe Painter who became rich when he rediscovered a mysterious gold mine on Gozo, Malta's sister island, which was lost since it was closed down in 1803. He died shortly afterwards and left his new found riches to the love of his life; his pet cat. I took the story with a pinch of salt, but it was told well.

"I've been sitting at your bar for the last two nights and don't know your name. What do people call you?" I asked, feeling the need to go out on a limb.

"Oskar."

"Oskar, I'm Gavin," I said, giving him my alias name. We shook hands, "you've got some great stories. You're a nice guy and I feel bad about lying to you yesterday. You see, I'm not really a fisherman."

"Oh?" he said frowning at me.

"You see, I'm a private investigator. I'm on the island to find a six year old Indian girl, who disappeared from England."

"Where do you think she is?" Oskar asked.

"I don't know."

"Is that the sort of thing you normally deal with?"

"No, not at all. My work normally involves cases of fraud or infidelity."

"Well, for what it's worth there are rumours of a powerful drug cartel that operates on the island."

"Interesting. What have you heard?"

"They say the cartel uses slave labour. People have been disappearing for years from across the island," Oskar explained. "They can be ruthless when threatened. There is one chilling incident that involved the mayor of a town in northern Malta, called Rabat. Five years ago, Alfred Pace proposed a series of tough measures aimed at stopping the illegal export of firearms and drugs. You see, his father had been shot down in the street years before and he wanted his revenge on the cartel."

"Okay," I said.

"Soon afterward this, on a sunny afternoon, Alfred was making a speech to a gathering of a hundred men, women and children outside a local hospital, where he was officially opening a new burns unit. He stood there with his large scissors next to the red ribbon across the new entrance, when a junkie pushed through the crowd and threw a vat of acid over his head. The acid etched into his face, hair and clothes leaving him in agony on the step. I've never heard a man scream so much."

"You were there?" I asked.

"Oh yes. Poor Alfred died that night, in the very hospital department he was opening. The acid burnt his lungs out," he recounted soberly. "The junkie was arrested, but never talked. I think he's still rotting in some jail. It must have been the cartel who put him up to it. If I were you, I would think very carefully before digging around too much."

◊◊◊

That evening, I arrived early to check out the building opposite the restaurant for any changes or signs of movement. Unfortunately nothing had altered: the lights were still out, the net curtains hadn't been moved and even the wrinkled crisp packet was still trapped under the back door.

Never mind. I was looking forward to the prospect of earning some much needed money and meeting Autumn again. She smiled as I entered the restaurant, which was still closed to customers. She looked as lovely as she had the day before, with her uniform hugging her curved body. I revealed the box of chocolates from behind my back, which brought on an infectious grin from her.

"Oh, Gavin. Thanks so much. That's very sweet of you," she said shyly.

"Thank you for helping me get this job," I said.

She put down the spare utensils on a table to take the chocolates from me, before giving me a peck on the cheek, still glowing with embarrassment.

I left her to finish laying the twenty tables in the dining area as I went to, what turned out to be, a quaint and very efficiently laid out kitchen, which was dominated by a large ivory and chrome coloured range cooker, with all five gas hobs blazing fiercely under pots and pans. Alongside was a multi-levelled stainless steel table, which had scratches from years of use, holding a stack of plates and cooking accessories.

I briefly introduced myself to the chef, who was a muscular fellow with the white toque, chef's jacket and stained drawstring pants. Despite his appearance, judging by the bouquet of aromas, he seemed to be doing a superb job of orchestrating the cooking. He acknowledged my presence with a grunt, and pointed me towards a side room, which was both the pantry and staff changing area.

Tinned and boxed goods were stacked neatly on industrial looking racking. On the bottom shelf at the side was a box of clothes, which after some forging, I was able to transform into a waiter, complete with black trousers, white shirt, waistcoat and a bow tie.

I stepped back through the steam and heat of the kitchen and returned to the seating area. Autumn was just lighting the candles on each of the tables, as it was dusk outside.

"How can I help?" I offered.

The front door opened at that moment, revealing a party of four.

"We've got customers," she whispered, "please take the chocolates and hide them in the kitchen." She bounded over to greet the arrivals.

I took the chocolate box from a table and stared ahead out of the full height front window at the darkened house opposite. Minutes later I was welcoming my first customer of the evening, an elderly lady, who wore pearls and a full length dress. I knew nothing about fashion but thought she was overdressed for the venue.

"Good evening, Madam. Do you have a reservation?" I asked as I smiled politely.

"Of course I don't. I never reserve."

"Umm. Sorry Madam," I stammered.

"You're new here, aren't you? Just you remember that I'm your best customer. I sit where I want. Tonight, I fancy a window seat."

"Certainly Madam. Please follow me," I said while cursing the old hag under my breath. I led her to the corner table by the front window. "Will this table suit you Madam?"

"Yes. What are the specials tonight?"

"Rosemary braised lamb shanks with roasted garlic, cream spinach and mashed potato," I said, while glancing at the specials board.

"No, sounds awful. I'll have the grilled salmon with new potatoes, carrots cooked in herbs and butter and a large glass of La Torre Girgentina. That's all," she barked.

I walked to the kitchen before writing the order, placing the slip on the counter and rang the bell just for the hell of it, as the chef had already seen me coming.

Autumn walked through the swing doors into the kitchen, with a grimace on her face.

"You've just had the pleasure of meeting the Dragun Mara."

"The what?"

"Dragon Lady," she whispered, with a cheeky grin.

"Yep. She's a bit of a beast."

"You get used to her."

"I don't know why I should have to."

"She certainly doesn't tip well, but she's friends with the manager, so you'll have to learn to cope with her. Also, you should put her Girgentina in a cold glass. She's fussy about that."

"How did you know she ordered Girgentina?" I asked.

"She orders it every night, with the salmon," Autumn said.

"Right, I better go and serve the dragon lady then." I said and left the kitchen to pour an extra large glass of white wine at the bar, before delivering it to my self-important customer, with a professional and courteous smile.

"Is there anything else I can bring before your dinner is ready?"

"Just my dinner," she said sharply.

I ignored the attitude and stepped away from the table, leaving her to stare out the window. As the sun set, the restaurant got busier and I found myself struggling to keep on top of my chores and the customer's requests.

Peppi arrived and gave me some stern words, to ensure his exacting standards were being achieved. I think he saw through my little ruse very quickly, as everything I did felt clunky and awkward. It must have been so obvious to that I was far from a high calibre waiter. I'd been naive to an extreme, it turned out that the service industry was actually very challenging.

As I moped up a spillage of orange juice from under table six, I glanced outside again to see nothing but darkness. The house was still empty. If the criminals just used it for cover passports then it may never be occupied or even visited. Maybe I was wasting my time.

"I want some apple pie," the Dragon Lady ordered, "and make it quick. The service tonight is appalling."

"Certainly." I said and turned to the kitchen where I returned the dirty mop and cut a piece of the chef's cinnamon deep filled apple pie, complete with thick glazed pastry. I plated it neatly and returned within sixty seconds with the mouth-watering dessert.

"Take it back. I want double cream with it."

"I will bring you some out."

"No. Listen. Take it away and give me some new apple pie with double cream."

"I don't see why you need a new dessert. I'll just bring some cream now."

"You'll take this away now," she fussed loudly, as she held the plate out at me.

I was enraged by her rudeness, but understood the general concept that the customer is always right. I disagreed with her logic, but nevertheless I took the plate back to the kitchen to fetch some cream. I returned with the same plate and the cream in a pouring jug. I placed the apple pie down on the table once more.

Just at that moment, I noticed a light turn on in the building opposite. I froze with the jug of cream in my hand, as I tried to peered out of the window, which was difficult because of the lights inside the restaurant. I moved quickly to the window and pressed my head against it.

"I said I want a new apple pie. Listen," she spat.

I squinted through and noticed that the light was emanating from a little window next to the front door, and there was a silhouette of a man inside.

"What are you doing? Come back here," she called to me.

I decided in that split second that my priority was to get across to the building as soon as possible, nothing else mattered. I also knew that Peppi would likely fire me by the end of the night. I looked across at Autumn and smiled at her. I figured I'd do her a favour before I left.

I returned to the Dragon Lady and held the cream above her head and poured. The cream flowed both down her face and the back of her head like a viscous, slow moving, waterfall.

"What are you bloody doing!" she screamed as she swerved her body, but I coolly followed her head till most the cream covered her.

It oozed between the pearls on her necklace, beneath her red cardigan and down the back of her neck. The restaurant fell silent as everyone goggled the unfolding drama in complete disbelief. Autumn froze and turned pale. Peppi was in the kitchen and oblivious to the assault at this point. I slammed the jug on the table.

"You're a rude old women. We don't want you in our restaurant ever again," I said sternly.

"You can't do that," she muttered.

"I already have," I quickly retorted and walked towards the door.

"You creep. Where's Peppi? You ruined my clothes!"

I turned to Autumn, whose gaze turned to a smirk. It was then I noticed Peppi stood by the kitchen door, visibly red with anger and wide eyed. The old dragon in the corner mopped her head with a serviette. I was satisfied that her fire had been quenched for good. Peppi went over to her aid. The initial shock faded as a faint chatter rippled through the restaurant.

"Peppi, I resign. Give her my wages for tonight, to cover her dry-cleaning," I said dryly.

"Get out." Peppi whispered sharply, as he held a cream soaked serviette.

Every customer watched as I slipped away, into the unlit street.

I crossed over into the shadows and waited by the front door of the property. I could make out movement on the inside of the building, by the front door.

The door opened and I made eye contact with a man in his late twenties, who was well built and dressed in black from head to toe. I looked away straight away and glanced at my watch.

He closed the door, locked it and turned to confront me.

"What are you doing?" he asked.

"Me? Err, nothing. I'm waiting for a friend," I said.

He pushed me in the chest. I walked away, round the corner, but he followed. He pushed me again from behind, so I turned to stand my ground.

"Get off me," I protested.

He revealed a knife in one of his hands. My heart raced, adrenaline surged and I became very aware of everything that happened next. I grabbed his arm and we wrestle for a moment. He was strong, but I used my superior body weight to push him backwards, he tripped on something and I ended up sitting on top of the thug, who was face down on the cobbled stone pavement. One of his arms was now under his body, while my hands had clenched his knife arm like a vice, restraining his movement.

"Get off me," he cried.

I didn't want to stand, as this would have enabled him to take another jab with the flick-knife, but I couldn't stay sitting on him all night. I needed some way to incapacitate him, so I could get away safely. It occurred to me that my diabetes may offer a solution. I reached into my side pocket with one hand and took out my insulin injection.

I twisted the dial to the maximum dose and stabbed him in the upper leg, which caused him to squeal, then pressed the button to inject the medicine into him, which I hoped would lower his blood sugar to dangerous levels.

The punk thrashed around for a couple of minutes, with occasional grunting, before his movements eased and he began twitching. His breathing became shallow and he fell unconscious. At this point, I took out a glucose gel, pulled down his lower lip and rubbed a dollop into his gums. The sugar boost would bring him round, as I didn't want to kill the guy!

Eighteen

I returned to my hotel shaken, but determined to get into the property. I asked Oskar to order a set of hook lock picks and a tension wrench from a supplier advertised on the internet. A few days later I collected the thin metallic objects in their presentation leather pouch from him. They looked more like dentist tools for removing plaque than an alternative to a key.

I had once been very familiar with the use of lock picks, forcing myself to remain supple in the dark art, in case my demanding clients required the skill. I practised on a selection of different locks that a carpenter client had installed into a single plank of wood for me as partial payment for a job. I had been able to work through the eight different locks in just under seven minutes. That was a long time ago though and I was rusty, but convinced myself it would be fine.

After passing the time till the early hours of a Wednesday morning with an old Western movie, I turned off the television and picked up my trench coat. I took a couple of sips from a bottle of whiskey and deliberately spilled some more onto the outside of the coat. This wasn't an act of insanity, or a waste of alcohol, but part of the plan. The thugs were obviously highly strung, so I wanted to give the impression to anybody who may have taken an interest in me, that I was no threat to anybody; simply a drunk meandering the streets.

I had my lock pick set and torch inside my coat pocket. I made my way out of the hotel and down the darkened streets, deliberately stumbling and swerving slightly, to live my cover. The narrow darkened streets with the tall city walls were claustrophobic and I felt vulnerable to another attack, but continued to the building of interest. I removed my whiskey bottle from my coat and leaned against the wall, pretending to swig from it, but actually looking both ways. I saw and heard nothing. It seemed that every soul in Valletta was asleep, except me.

I stumbled to the front door and leaned against it. I quickly installed the tension wrench into the base of the deadbolt and then began working on the top pins, pushing them up one at a time. For the next five minutes I muttered aggressively under my breath, as a drunk may do, to dissuade anybody from approaching me. I was clearly out of practise, as I caught and then dropped the layers of pins in the lock. On occasion, I took out the by now half empty bottle of whiskey and raised it to my lips as I turned to check if anybody was watching.

I was far from a professional in this delicate work, but understood the basics. All the pins had to be raised to the right level, to allow the bolt to turn freely. Eventually there was a highly satisfying click as the deadbolt glided back inside the door. I moved next to the latch lock, which I managed after only a minute or so. I slipped on some latex surgical gloves I'd bought from a pharmacy and turned the handle.

A moment of acute nervousness overcame me at this point, as this was a critical stage of the operation; once I crossed the threshold of the front door, my alibi of being a benign drunk was no longer believable. My true intentions, to break into the property, could be seen by anybody walking passed.

I was also all too aware that this address was the only clue I'd collected, almost two weeks previously. It had to lead to something of significance, or everything I'd endured to get to this point would have been in vain.

Following one final glance over my shoulder, I pushed opened the door, which was heavier than expected, but my higher than usual adrenaline levels ensured I managed the task with ease. I floundered into something that rustled as I pulled my feet through it to get inside. I closed the door and stood in total darkness on the doormat as I reached for my torch.

The torch beam revealed a pile of post on the side of the doormat, about a foot high at the peak and spilled down the corridor. I sifted through the post, most of which were flyers for pizza delivery companies and Chinese restaurants. Junk mail seemed to be as common a blight in Malta as it was in the UK.

The building was not quite as grand inside as it appeared from the street. It must have been inhabited for quite some years, judging by the strings of cobwebs that interweaved the wooden posts that made up the staircase at the end of the corridor. There was a hole in the centre point of the hallway ceiling with an elaborative ceiling rose around it, hinting at the extravagant chandelier that must have once hung from that point.

The paint on the walls had peeled in places and there was a smell of damp. I imagined that an estate agent may describe the period property as *'having great potential, but in need of complete modernisation'*.

I walked into the kitchen through one of the side doors, to find a wood burning wrought iron stove and large old fashioned kitchen island in the centre of the room, surrounded by soiled black and white chequered paved flagstones. There was a large sitting room opposite the kitchen, with a chimney and hearth. Neither of these rooms contained any furniture aside from what was built into the house.

I was disheartened by the lack of clues on the ground floor, but continued upstairs. There were four bedrooms and two grimy bathrooms, all empty.

On my way back down the staircase, I noticed a single smoke alarm sensor unit in the top right of the corridor, positioned on the wall facing down the corridor. I found this weird for a number of reasons, firstly, it was the newest thing in an otherwise dated house. Secondly, I hadn't seen any other smoke sensors in the rest of the house and thirdly, it was installed at the top of the wall rather than on the ceiling as smoke sensors should be. Admittedly it could have been installed incorrectly, but it still roused my curiosity.

I reached across the banisters halfway down the stairs and wiped my finger across the device. It was perfectly clean and free from all cobwebs and dust, and so must have been installed fairly recently. My torch revealed a small hole in the centre of the test button. I was very familiar with the concept of covert camera systems and had deployed such devices myself for clients in the past. Most were standalone units that could easily be installed and captured video or still images.

I lifted the detector from the wall and inched it away carefully, but stopped as I noticed two wires going into a hole in the wall directly behind; one thick white and a thinner black one. This confirmed that this was no ordinary smoke detector, as commercially available devices of this sort were battery operated, but this one looked identical from the front, but had wires at the rear.

I knew what this meant instantly. Someone was very serious about monitoring this building, discreetly. I carefully replaced the detector exactly and covered the camera aperture with a tissue from my pocket before returning to the front door. From there, I shone the torch back and confirmed that the camera was perfectly positioned to take an image of anybody entering through the front door.

The thicker white cable coming out of the back of the unit was likely to provide power, so the unit could operate without maintenance for long durations. The second thinner wire caused me concern. I took some deep breaths.

I dropped to the floor by the front door and frantically shovelled the hundreds of letters and flyers aside with my hands away from the door. I gripped the corner of the ragged old carpet and pulled it up. There were no pressure sensors on the concrete floor that lay underneath. I next ran my finger along the side of the door frame all the way around. Also nothing.

This was a problem, because the second thinner cable appeared not to be a trigger input to operate the camera. The most common such trigger for such a camera would most likely have been mounted by the front door. The lack of a trigger was worrying me as this meant the cable was most likely a live feed, that went either to a recording device or a remote television that someone could be monitoring.

I was paralysed by indecision. I sat on the pile of post by the door and thought, weighing up my options. I jumped to my feet but the fumes of the whiskey made me sway slightly.

If someone happened to have been watching the live feed from the concealed smoke detector camera at that moment, then they would have seen an obscured image, caused by the tissue placed over the lens. My actions would have already revealed to any observer that I had identified that a camera existed. I had inadvertently, and rather stupidly revealed a lot about my own capabilities in the process of searching the house. Damn.

I was acutely aware that a group of highly motivated assassins could have been racing to the building at that very moment. I needed to act fast, whatever I decided to do. Should I simply leave, or could I still salvage something from this situation to make it appear to be an attempted burglary? I doubted anything would matter now. I found myself staring at the mound of junk mail that was spewed across the carpet.

Aware that the thug from last night could arrive at any moment. I picked through the copious amounts of pizza discount vouchers and double glazing flyers and took two or three envelopes that stood out. My final act, before fleeing, was to kick the carpet back down and remove the tissue from the camera. I pulled the door shut, turned off the torch and melted into the darkness of the street.

I quickly crossed the road and walked by the restaurant and down a side street. My heart rate rose as I suddenly heard someone running very fast down the adjacent street towards the building. I stopped in my tracks and stepped into the nearest shop doorstep, which was a florist. The running turned to walking and got fainter. I had to be brave as this was possibly my best opportunity to identify someone associated with the group. I stepped out from the shop and tiptoed back to the corner of the building and poked my head round to see the front door of the building was wide open and the downstairs light was on.

I held my breath, not knowing exactly what to do. I knew that whoever had been monitoring the camera was located someone close by and I had heard the direction they had run from. I knew it was too risky to stay where I was and watch them when they left the property, so I backed away, passed by the florist again and turned left at the next junction, towards the adjacent street where I'd first heard the runner.

Now, given it had been ten minutes since my arrival in the house and the fact that they had sprinted to the house, I assessed it was unlikely that they had been sprinting for the whole duration, as no one other than an Olympic runner could manage such a feat. Far more likely was the possibility that they had driven here and only sprinted the last few hundred metres.

Reassuming my drunken persona, I swerved down the road stumbling between the cars and placing a hand on their bonnets to check the temperature. A car bonnet heats up quite quickly, even after just a short drive. I also listened carefully as I went along, for two very important noises; steps behind me and for the distinctive ticking of a cooling car radiator.

Three cars ahead, I noticed a strange orange light appear behind the windscreen and then disappear just as quickly. I stopped at the side of a car and reached into my pocket for my almost empty whiskey. The orange appeared again and my heart sunk, as I realised it was the ember of a lit cigarette that was being inhaled by a man sat in the darkness of a car, most likely while he waited for somebody, maybe his partner in crime, who was at that moment in the property?

I'd little choice but to go deep into character. I swigged the bottle, stumbled back onto the pavement and leaned against the window of a closed tapas bar. In the stillness of the empty street I couldn't see who sat in the cab, but knew they were spying on me. I started to walk again towards the car, as I had little option but to continue. The driver side window lowered and the man flicked his cigarette onto the road.

I felt his eyes burn into me with suspicion. I kept walking slowly, holding my bottle. I could read his number plate as I came alongside the car in front, 'KTE 634'. His door opened and the car interior light came on to reveal a square-jawed, bald, well built man. I had to do something special, and quickly, to divert his attention away from me. As he stepped out, he took his eyes off me for a second and I took the opportunity to put my fingers down my throat. The combination of the whiskey smell, my fear and fingers were enough to make me throw up onto the pavement. I added some extra sound effects, to exaggerate my apparent condition.

'Eugh!' I heard him mutter and he returned to his seat.

I wasn't proud, but think I narrowly avoided an even more unpleasant experience. I stumbled to the next corner, and as soon as I was out of sight, ran as fast as my unfit body would allow, which was a lot further than I thought possible, probably because I was motivated by fear. I switched to walking at the point where my knees almost buckled and my lungs felt like they were going to collapse. I dragged my exhausted carcass back towards my hotel.

After I had walked a couple of laps round the hotel, to ensure I wasn't being followed, I went into the hotel and collapsed in my room. While still heaving for breath from the exertions of the evening, I leaned across from my bed to scribble the number plate on the top of some hotel notepaper and threw my booze stained clothing into the bathroom.

The fear subsided and was replaced by anger. The house had been a trap and was obviously just used to provide a cover address. I had walked straight into the trap. Stupid.

Remembering the post I had stolen, I returned to my coat and ripped open the letters. The first two envelopes were addressed to 'the occupier' and were just junk mail from a credit card company. There were no account details or names in the content. In disgust I scrunched them up and threw them in the direction of the bin.

The final envelope was entitled to 'Franka Inkorporati'. I opened it to find what looked like a tax statement from the 'Commissioner of Inland Revenue', with a large number of financial figures and deductions and other wording in Maltese. There was a final sum at the bottom of the page of the order of three million Euros. This seemed like a very healthy amount of money to be associated with such a dilapidated house. They had been busy, but thankfully for me, it looked like they had been sloppy and not collected their statement straight away. Maybe that was why they had been keen to get to the house so quickly.

I collapsed again on my bed with exhaustion, but thrilled to finally, against all odds, have some solid evidence, even though I was unsure what it meant.

Nineteen

When I awoke the following morning, I wondered how best to exploit what I'd discovered the night before. With a clear head I grasped the single A4 sheet tax statement from the bedside table and read it again for further clues. I was convinced the statement would help prove that *'Franka Inkorporati'* was just a front company, that was being used by the criminal gang to launder stolen money; to make illegally gained money clean again.

I guessed that *'Inkorporati'* must mean incorporated, but needed to confirm this. If the company was incorporated, then I hoped this meant it would be registered with a Maltese government body. I knew that British companies had to be registered and suspected the same regulation applied in Malta. If this were the case then I hoped there might be some publically available information about the company to identify the company senior management and alternative premises. My hope was that Dipa was being held at a location controlled by this front company. Of course, I didn't yet have proof, so it was merely speculation at that time.

I was hit by the overpowering stench of whiskey as I opened the bathroom door. I scrubbed my clothes and dried them in the sunshine over the Juliet balcony, while I showered. Half an hour later, my clothes were dry and I was ready to leave the hotel.

I grabbed the note with the licence plate on it. It was reassuringly difficult to find a vehicle owner's name from the licence plate in the UK, and with none of my usual contacts to approach, I suspected it would be a difficult task to track a Maltese car.

I headed to the nearest internet cafe and instead focussed my efforts on locating the front company. I shouldn't have been surprised to discover that none of the English websites in the search results were relevant, but there were lots in either Maltese or Greek; both languages were equally alien to me. I was somewhat disheartened as I had little confidence that any of the online translation services would be accurate enough to help. I was however fairly sure that the company's name translated to be 'Limestone Incorporated'.

It occurred to me that Autumn would be the perfect person to assist me with this problem, as I remembered she was studying Maltese business. I paid for my time on the computer and walked towards the restaurant, aware that I was risking bumping into the thugs again, but it was daylight and my appearance was different, so felt it was worth the risk.

I saw Autumn through the window as I approached from outside. She was serving coffee to a man, so I knocked on the window after she was done. She looked at me blankly and stepped outside onto the street.

"What the hell are you doing here?" she said.

"Hello. I wanted to see you."

"You're an idiot. Why did you do that last night?" she asked.

"The lady was being so rude. I thought..." I started.

"Is that what you do to everyone who is rude to you? I almost lost my job because of you. Peppi trusted my judgement, when I recommended he take you on."

"I'm really sorry," I said, to try dissolve the tension. There was a long pause as she considered how to react.

"What do you want? You know he won't take you back".

Just then I noticed two men walk towards the building opposite carrying large bags. They looked like workmen, as they wore paint stained t-shirts and dirty old trainers. I stared as they pushed open the front door and stepped inside.

"I'm over here, Gavin," she said, as she stood with her hands on her hips. I turned to face her.

"Sorry," I said again, as I refocused on her, "Well, you see, I'm a private investigator and I really need your help."

"A what?" she said in disbelieve.

"I have a document," I said, as I unfolded the tax statement to show her, "and I need your help to understand what it is."

"Where did you get this, Gavin?"

"That's not important. I remember that you are studying business studies at college, so you can translate this thing for me, please Autumn?" I begged.

I placed it into her hands and she gripped it and began to read. I glanced back at the men, who had the front door open and had laid cable along the narrow pavement. Autumn looked confused.

"It's a tax statement for a private company, but there are a huge number of losses for last year. The company is just below the minimum tax threshold. Are you investigating this company, Gavin?"

"Yes. Are there any other details I need to know?"

"Details of the directors of the company?" she asked.

I nodded, as I had noted a list of names on the sheet, but didn't know who they were. "Yes, please."

"The executive director is Leon Dingli."

"Thank you so much," I said.

"I've got to get back to work now. I guess this is goodbye then," she said.

"Not yet. I'd like to get a coffee please?"

"Really? Peppi will kill you if he finds you in his restaurant again. There are plenty of other coffee shops you could go."

"Is he here now?" I asked.

"No, but..."

I ignored her and sat myself at a window seat. I stared out at the workers. Autumn followed, clearly annoyed by my rudeness, but I had a great opportunity.

"What are you looking at? Those men?" she spat.

"Yes. I promise to leave after my coffee and you'll never see me again. I'm sorry I lied to you."

She returned with a coffee and the bill, which she threw onto the table before spilling the coffee.

"Drink up and leave," she ordered, "I've had enough of your games."

The men appeared to be installing some electrical system into the house. One man had returned with a long ladder and had begun to nail a wire along the brickwork underneath the top floor window ledge, which left an exposed wire dangling in the air. He then drilled a hole into the wooden window frame of an adjoining window and fed the cable through, before coming down from the ladder.

Another man later appeared at the top floor window with a drill and attached a bracket underneath the window with the exposed wire. The workman then skilfully attached the exposed wire to the rear of a camera unit and fixed it to the wall bracket.

I chuckled at the thought that I'd spooked them the other night into upgrading their security. Having observed the workmen for almost an hour, I was confident they were professional electricians and nothing more. They didn't care about people walking past and were not carrying weapons. I formulated a plan.

I left a generous tip for Autumn and waved from across the room as I left. Predictably, and probably quite justifiably, she ignored me, but I couldn't be distracted by her anymore. I timed my exit to coincide with one of the men stepping outside. I walked over.

"Hi. I wanted to ask you something?" I said, making sure I wasn't standing in line with the front door, as I knew the camera in the hallway would still be active, and the front door was wide open. The workman came over. He had tattoos on his arms and beads of sweat on his brow.

"Yep," he said simply.

"I'm thinking of getting a camera system installed at my house. How much do you charge?" I asked.

"It depends on the system you want."

"I have a house like this one. What system are you putting in here?"

"This is a big job. Lots of cameras with a remote feed. It's quite pricey, but we do smaller installations too. Where do you live?"

"Not far away. Do you have a business card?"

"I've got one in the van," he said and started walking down a side street.

"Have you got the name of the owners of this place? It would be nice to ask them about the system," I asked as we approached a white van.

"Sorry, I can't disclose customer information," he said as he reached through the open front window to a business card box on the dashboard. "Here you go," he handed a card across, with the business name, '*Cameras & Sensors*', address and telephone number.

I noted the open window and the edge of some papers on the front seat of the van, which were partly concealed by a lads magazine, featuring a busty blonde draped across a car on the cover.

"Thanks for your help. I'll be in touch soon," I said and walked partly down the street.

I looked back over my shoulder to see the workman had gone from the van, so I returned quickly and snatched the papers from underneath the magazine on the front seat. It was clearly a list of jobs for the week. I walked to the back of the van and flicked through to their schedule for that day. I found myself staring at the name, telephone number and address of the customer for the installation.

I scribbled the details down in my notebook, before returning the papers to the van. I walked away, thrilled that the plan had worked better than expected, as I'd expected to have to break into the company's premises to get the customer's details later that night.

Twenty

The name on the customer paperwork was Leon Dingli. Bingo. I had a match with the name on the tax statement. Next to the name it read *'Magna Metallis'*, whatever that meant. Most importantly, I had an address: *'1 Lito, Genejna'*. I finally had the name of someone linked to this whole bloody mess. It might have been reckless, but I'd wasted enough time on the island and saw no reason to wait any longer. With a simple cover story in mind, one of a freelance journalist, I hailed a taxi and gave the driver the address. I had played the journalist cover before for a job and it worked well, so I was confident of deploying it again.

The cab arrived forty-five minutes later at a remote location, about a kilometre from the shore, just south of Genejna, in the north-west of the island. There was a perimeter fence around what appeared to be nothing more than overgrown and rugged rolling scrublands. There was a tall watchtower positioned near the entrance, but asked the taxi driver to drop me some distance away. A large yellow sign positioned behind the fence stood ten feet high and read *'Magna Metallis'* in black letters. Below the letters there was a simple picture of a working quarry with trucks.

I walked along the fence, towards the tower about four hundred metres ahead. A man was perched at the top with a pair of binoculars trained on me. There were small signs hanging at regular intervals on the fence that read *'Danger, Explosives'* and a simple cartoon of explosives detonating. There was a well worn path on the inside of the perimeter where I thought guards patrolled, some with dogs, judging by the smelly deposits that the flies had been attracted to.

The taxi was halfway to the horizon in no time at all. There were no other buildings or cars in any direction, just barren landscape and the road which led to the sea in one direction and humanity in the other. There was no way of approaching this place stealthily because of the remote location, flat landscape and tall watchtower. The owners were serious about keeping people off their land, which suggested there was more to the company than simply mining.

I Rather disturbingly, a guard in a brown uniform stepped out from the base of the tower and headed towards me. As he got closer I waved.

"Hello there. Do you speak English?" I yelled.

"Yes. Can I help you?" the man said after he got closer.

"Please can I see Mr. Dingli. My name's Gavin Whittaker," I said.

"Come this way," the guard said and escorted me towards the reception, at the base of the tower.

"What does Magna Metallis mean?" I asked thumbing at the sign.

"Grand Mines. Does Mr. Dingli know you're coming?"

"No."

We walked into the reception area and the guard spoke to the receptionist, in what I thought was Greek. She in turn picked up the phone and made a call. All I could understand of the call was my name and the word 'english'. She hung up and smiled at me.

"Mr. Dingli is on his way," she said in a soothing voice, "please take a seat."

I remained standing simply because I was nervous as hell. I needed to keep sharp. After a very long ten minutes, I heard a car approach the building from the opposite side of the fence and stop. The door slammed and the back door of the building opened to reveal an elderly gentleman who wore a perfectly tailored double-breasted charcoal suit with a well groomed moustache.

"Good afternoon Sir. I'm Leon Dingli, but please call me Leon," he said and offered his hand. I noticed the top two-thirds of his forefinger was missing, but his grip was still firm.

"Gavin Whittaker. Nice to meet you."

"How can I help you?"

"I'm a freelance writer and am writing a piece about the Maltese mineral markets. I was hoping to get some expert insight for my article, if you could please help?" I said, spinning a line.

"That sounds interesting. I'd be delighted to help. Please come with me and we can have a chat now," he said and led me out the back. I was a little surprised that he was so willing, and strangely it came across as if he was almost eager to help. Before I knew it, I'd been escorted through to the other side of the reception area and out of the door and was sat in a jeep. Leon drove us into the scrubland, without any fuss or further conversation, which worried me.

Despite is age, Leon drove quickly and seemed very alert. I noticed that he had a perfectly groomed white head of hair, swept to the side, and contained no receding patches. His face was tanned, but with few sunspots and his skin looked well moisturised. He clearly looked after himself.

"Nice place you have," I offered.

"Thank you. This mine produces a million cubic metres of soft limestone every year, most of which is exported," he said dryly, "let's wait till we get to my office before we start."

We arrived at the top of an incline that led underground. Leon stopped the car and we walked down into the rock and round a corner to a discreet entrance, which appeared to be a lift that had been built into what I imagined to be an old mine shaft.

The lift was already open to us, so we walked straight into the cage. Leon pulled the two scissor gate doors shut and lowered a large lever. The lift juddered to life and trundled downwards. Daylight was replaced by weak artificial light. The temperature dropped as we descending. A wall of solid yellow rock appeared to travel upwards on the other side of the scissor gate before it suddenly disappeared and a bright light pierced through. The lift stopped. He unclipped and heaved open the gates, to reveal a quite unexpected level of luxury, which was the opposite end of the spectrum to the caveman domain I'd anticipated.

"Please come in," he said as he stepped out of the industrial lift.

"Wow," I gawked as I slowly placed one of my grubby shoes onto the thick plush cream carpet that spread across the floor of the underground lair.

"Don't worry about any mess. I have cleaners who will get it out," he said, clearly sensing my hesitation.

The place had the feel of an expensive hotel, with tessellating gold and teal wallpaper, shimmering where the full spectrum light from the sunken halogen lighting system reflected the pattern. There were also fine, water coloured landscapes spaced evenly along the lengthy corridor ahead. There were two men and a woman in smart casual attire, who walked purposefully through the hallway as made our way.

"Not far now," he said.

The corridor was littered with doors on both sides, and at least two additional passageways which diverted at right angles. Leon led us down one of these turns and I noted another two diverting corridors. He walked at a regular pace, swinging his arms slightly too far on each step, like he was trying not to march; maybe he was in the military before joining civvy street?

I peeked into two rooms on our travels, one was a regular office and the other a large storeroom containing boxes upon boxes. All in all, it was a vast complex. I felt very cut off down there and nervous, as this certainly didn't feel like an ordinary office for an ordinary business. What the hell had I found?

I thought of what Oskar had told me about the extensive underground bunker networks that were created during the Second World War. Maybe that lair was part of the same network? We eventually turned right into a large office suite which wouldn't have been out of place for a prestigious oil tycoon. It had ample space for entertaining, lounging and working, with a double height ceiling, unique furniture, including a hanging oak finished spherical seat, dangling by cables between three seven foot stands; completely impractical, but a fantastic talking point.

"Would you like a cup of something before we begin? Maybe tea? You English love your tea."

"No, thank you," I said, feeling apprehensive about the conversation ahead.

"Please make yourself at home," Leon said, offering a seat in the office area of the room.

I walked gingerly across a tiger skin rug, which I hoped was fake until I spotted the head, and reclined into a single seat leather sofa and let it swallow me up. Leon opted for the double seated version opposite. Next to him was a large swanky glass coffee table that had consumed part of a leather upholstered Ferrari dashboard, complete with steering wheel and prancing horse badge. On top of this impressive centrepiece were copies of various international newspapers, including 'The Times'.

"I enjoy the quality journalism, whatever the source," he said, "now, tell me why you *think* you are here."

"Why I *think* I am here?" I asked, wondering if he was playing some sort of psychological trick on me.

"Yes. Please tell me."

My carefully prepared opening lines instantly evaporated by that bamboozling question. What did he know that I didn't? He completely threw me.

"I'm a reporter and am writing a-" I started.

"No you're not and no you aren't," he interrupted. "Come on, you can do better than that." Leon interrupted.

"What?" I asked. Leon took out a cigar and Zippo lighter from his inside jacket pocket and lit up.

"I wanted to ask you some questions," I said carefully.

"Okay. I'm all ears," he said, "what do you want to know?"

I thought carefully.

"I tell you what," he continued, "come over here and see if any of these documents answer your questions."

Leon struggled to get himself out of his chair with his one good hand, before putting the cigar in his mouth and pushing himself up with both instead. We walked to the other side of the office, past the pond built into the floor, containing two fat and inactive coy fish and towards an oak sculptured antique bureau, where a pile of papers were stacked over the dark green leather desktop inlay.

"Please have a read," Leon instructed, pointing to the papers. "All your answers can be found here."

I didn't know what was happening or why, but I picked up the top sheet of paper and read.

"Please have a seat," he offered. I sat. "I think I'll have a Scotch. Do you want one, Joe?"

I flicked through the top document, which was written in Maltese but appeared to be a lease between the Maltese government and *'Magna Metallis'* on the use of the land at this location. The next set of documents were in English and outlined a business strategy forecast for the next five years. The document talked about *'company product'* and gave projections for *'demands within Europe'*. It all seemed very businesslike. Leon returned with two filled smoked glass tumblers.

"It's Scottish single malt whiskey, of course. I wouldn't want to kill you," he said wryly.

"You knew I was coming didn't you."

"I hoped you would," Leon said.

I flicked to the next document that contained a schematic of the tunnel network. It was far bigger than I'd appreciated from my brief visit. There were large open planned chasms further down the central tunnel and a medical bay, canteen, gym, cinema, shops, everything. If I had to compare the complex to anything, it would be to an ocean liner. Someone could live underground and never see sunlight again if you wanted. There were even sunbed stations to top up your Vitamin D levels.

"So, why am I here?"

"To help with my business, Joe Patterson," he said.

"What? How do you know my name?" I asked, puzzled before realising that it actually wasn't the first time he'd used it.

Cruelly, I was denied the opportunity to discover anything further as we were abruptly disturbed by distant screams and shouts from elsewhere in the complex. I gasped. Leon stood, but could do nothing as the door was thrown open and a police officer stormed the room. We were both arrested.

Twenty One

"And that's it, officer. You now know how I ended up here," I say to Inspector Bosco. "Can I please make a call to the British Embassy now?"

"Maybe. Although you've still not convinced me that you're innocent of anything. If you can't help us, then we can't help you. I'll give you one last chance, do you know Nicodemus?"

"No. Sorry," I shake my head while I try to look as sternly as possible. I can't risk telling him the truth.

"Are you sure? We can offer you protection, if you're afraid."

"No," I say, feeling bad that I'm lying to a police officer, but it is the only way. "Look this has been really stressful for me. I need to make a call to the embassy, please."

"I'll see what I can do. Sit tight," he says and disappears from the cell.

Once again, I sit alone, my wrists still hurting, as I mull over the conversation I never told Inspector Bosco...

"What? How do you know my name?" I asked Leon Dingli.

"It was a hunch. When the receptionist called and said there was a journalist here to see me, and his name was Gavin Whittaker, I thought to myself that name sounds familiar, so I looked it up before coming to meet you. It was on one of our passports that was stolen in the UK. I also knew that my men were hunting down a Brit called Joe Patterson, who they suspected of stealing the passport, so it wasn't that difficult to work you out," he said.

"Oh," is all I could mutter. The old man was smart.

"You first came to my attention when you caused problems for us in England. I wanted to speak with you, but you kept eluding my men. So, just imagine how delighted I am that you walked through my door today," Leon said as he cradled his whiskey in the palm of his hand. "Was it you who picked the front door of our Valletta office too?" he asked with only intrigue in his voice.

"I was just trying to find Dipa Sharma," I said.

"You're intriguing," he said and paused for thought. "Dipa's here. I'm not convinced whether there is more to your visit to Malta than just finding her though. You see, I know that you're a private investigator, and work for Greg Webber."

"I don't know what to say," I said, surprised by the direction of the conversation.

Leon swirled his drink, deep in thought. "I met Greg once you know. He was trying to take my customers from me here in Malta. I made it very clear to him that he had no right to operate in this country."

"Are you saying that Greg sells drugs? I think you've got him confused with someone else," I said in disbelief.

"Well, Mr. Webber uses his private investigations business as a front. His real passion lies in the heroin market. You see Greg and his associates have a large drug production network of their own," Leon continued as he strolled round the desk. "They are my main competitors in Europe. So Joe, why are you really here?" he asked pointedly, as he observed my reaction to the question.

"I'm only here to find Dipa. Nothing more," I said firmly.

"Then you've been used, Joe. I think you were doing Greg Webber's dirty work for him."

"How do you know this about Greg?"

"It's my job to know about my competitors," Leon said. "They're greedy and want to ruin my business."

"So you're a drug dealer then?" I asked.

"A dealer is someone at the end of the supply chain, who sells to the consumer. I enable both the supply and the delivery. I don't believe in middlemen, they're bad for business. I control the entire operation," he said grandly. I took my glass and sipped the whiskey. It was warming with an oaky taste. I took a few gulps and held my breath for a second, so I wouldn't cough.

"Where does Dipa fit into all of this?" I asked.

"Well, when diacetylmorphine was first synthesized in the 1870s, it was done on a small scale and relied on the extraction of the chemicals from opium poppy. This is a primitive and slow process. You have to wait for the poppy to grow and then harvest it. I've got some clever chemists who have sped the process up, so I can now produce tons of product very quickly. I need a large workforce to make this happen and because it's difficult to recruit for this line of work, I rely on a steady stream of people who are picked from the streets; people who won't be missed, or people who are sold to me. They all live and die underground, but we make them as comfortable as possible," Leon preached.

"So the fence around this place is really to keep the workers in?"

"Yes, and prying eyes out. It works most of the time," Leon said. "I'm glad you came though. I've got big plans for someone with your tenacity."

"Why would I ever work for you?"

"As you can imagine, I've some experience with motivating people to do what I want. Most parents' Achilles' heel is their offspring, and I suspect yours is no different. Your boy is called Stuart, isn't he?" Leon said, as he stared into my eyes.

I suddenly felt very hot and uncomfortable, "You won't hurt my son!"

"He's a very nice young man and I'm sure he does well at school. Why would I want to ruin that? Besides, there's the matter of the CCTV systems that have you logged strolling into our cover office in Valletta and also here, where you *willingly* shook my hand at the entrance. It's difficult to explain that evidence away. Then finally, of course, there are your fingerprints that are all over the company documents and footage from other cameras..." he said and pointed above the door to a discreet camera aimed at his desk, "That one captured you sitting at my desk, talking with the chairman of this drug factory. It looks to me like you've made yourself at home."

My blood boiled. I stood and walked round to square up to Leon. He was a short man. His tailor-made suit fitted perfectly, following the contours of his well-rounded midriff.

"You bastard. You stitched me up. What the hell do you want from me now?" I asked.

"Well, you see, I've got something of yours, if I choose to take him. To make things fair, to build trust between us, I'll give you something of mine. My name. I'm Nicodemus Antonelli. Mr. Dingli is just one of my alternative names, to keep my true identity a secret. So, now we're partners," he said, extending his hand. I shook it reluctantly.

"I guess I don't have a choice," I said.

"Two more things. Firstly, I expect you to never share my name with anyone else, especially not the police. If you were to ever do that, then I would end your son's life." Nicodemus said softly. "Secondly, I need you to shut down Mr. Webber's drug operations. Destroy him. Do you understand?" I nodded. "Once you have, then you have my personal guarantee that you and your son will never be harmed. You're only alive now because you're useful to me, despite all the problems you've caused."

"I'm confused though. If you know so much about Greg's dealings, why can't you just give the police an anonymous tip off?"

"That's very short sighted of you, Joe. I'm disappointed. It's always better for your enemies to never suspect you had anything to do with their demise. I want Mr. Webber to think he knows who it was that brought down his operations."

"So you're happy for him to think it was me?" I asked, disgusted by his attitude.

Nicodemus shrugged. "Yes. The only consolation for you is that Greg was equally happy to use you in the same way. At least I've got the balls to be honest with you."

"I'll do what you say, but I've got one condition. I came here to find Dipa and I want here returned to her family, alive and well."

"You're in no position to be making demands, but I find your dogged enthusiasm for the young girl charming. You know I have eighty two other workers in this bunker. Do you expect me to release them all?"

"Dipa's only six. She won't know where she was or what happened to her. You wouldn't miss someone so young."

"The young ones have small fingers, which are useful for some of the finer processes. They also have a longer work life. I get more use out of them."

"You talk about them as if they're animals."

"They're all here to fulfil a task. I don't take people I don't need. Look, I could make an exception with Dipa. I'll have someone look into whether she is too young to remember any important details. If it's possible, then she'll be released."

At this point the door burst open and the police stormed the room, handcuffing me and Nicodemus. I then had a linen blindfold tied round my head and the police said this was to stop me from communicating with anybody else while they evacuated us from the bunker. I heard others struggling and shouting. I was led to a car and driven for about an hour, still handcuffed and blindfolded. Eventually I was taken into a building, a lift and into a room, where the blindfold was finally removed.

Twenty Two

Inspector Bosco returns and closes the interview room door behind him. He sits and reads through his notes in silence. I hold the cup in my hand and sip some tepid water while staring ahead. I mop the perspiration from my brow.

"Can I call the embassy?" I ask.

The Inspector looks up slowly. "You sure you don't know anything about Mr. Nicodemus?" he asks.

"Nothing. I was there to find Dipa. I couldn't find her, so was going to leave. That's it. Can you help me now?"

"Okay, stand up please" he says and stands.

I stretch my legs out and then stand as well. He tilts his head to the side slightly "Congratulations. You passed the test," he says excitedly as he takes hold of my hand and shakes it firmly.

Err, what's going on? I briefly wonder whether he's having some sort of mental breakdown.

"Don't take it personally Joe," he says, still sniggering, as he walks to the door. He opens it to reveal Nicodemus standing outside. Weird, I think.

Nicodemus smiles at me and strolls in, patting the Inspector on the shoulder, who smiles at him like a Cheshire Cat. I'm confused as hell and sit back down. I feel like I'm the only one in the room not getting a punchline to a very funny joke.

"What the hell is going on?" I ask.

"You're not in a police station, Joe. I had to be sure, you see. You did great, even with my best interrogator. I know I can trust you now," Nicodemus says.

I put my hands up to my face. I can't cope. It had felt good to talk to someone after running for so long, almost therapeutic, but it's all been a lie. I'm devastated, but also relieved that I'm not in jail.

"Do you have any more games for me?" I snap, "I'm leaving."

"No one is stopping you, Joe. You're a free man. Here's some money to cover your expenses," he says and hands me an envelope full of money before waving me out.

I leave the hot room into a slightly larger and much cooler room. The interview room is completely contained inside the larger room, which also contains an industrial heater linked, with stainless steel flue piping, to the vent in the cell wall.

They had deliberately made me sweat. I open the larger room door to find a familiar luxurious corridor inside the bunker complex. It was even cooler out here, hidden under the earth. They had driven me around before bringing me blindfolded back to the same place. Cunning.

"Just remember what I told you. I'll have Dipa released when I know you've left Malta. See you around," Nicodemus calls as I walk down the corridor, towards the lift.

Nicodemus has been the mastermind behind everything. I'm furious and worse still, there seems to be nothing I can do, but follow his instructions.

I make my way up by lift and discover it's dark outside. I trek back across the arid landscape towards the watch tower, which now resembles a lighthouse, with light beams emanating from the structure that pierces the darkness and aids the guards with their continual search of the grounds. A wandering beam soon blinds me and sticks to me as a guard runs up and screams something in Maltese.

"English?" I ask, as I raise my arms in the air, hoping he understands this international language and doesn't shoot.

"Name?"

"Joe Patterson."

The guard speaks into his walkie-talkie and after a short burst of static gets a reply.

"Follow me," he orders.

The receptionist calls me a taxi while I sit in the waiting area. The car arrives and I hop in, taking a deep breath as the vehicle pulls away.

I still have my fake passport. As soon as I reach the hotel I purchase a one way plane ticket to London, leaving in the morning. Although flying by plane means passing through more security, I figure I'll take my chances since I've just survived one interrogation already. I head to '*The Zoltan*' bar for a tall cold beer.

"Hey, it's you," Oskar welcomes me as I walk through the door. "Did you find that girl?"

"Work in progress. It's been a hell of a day." I say and order my drink as I sit on a bar stool.

Oskar pours a cold one and slides it across the counter.

"I was thinking of you earlier today, as I walked through a bunker network in the north of the island," I say.

"Really? Whereabouts?"

A customer in the corner of the room starts coughing loudly. I turn to see a women stand and walk towards me, holding a glass. She's middle aged with mousy hair, wearing a t-shirt, shorts and flip-flops.

"Is he annoying you, Oskar?" she asks.

"No. He's fine Amanda."

"Be a sweetheart, Oskar. Go get me some ice from out back, for my drink," Amanda orders and sits on the stool next to mine. Oskar nods and disappears. She leans in close to my ear.

"Don't say anything stupid, Joe. Remember what you promised," she whispers.

She smiles as Oskar returns with ice and drops some cubes into her white wine spritzer.

"Thanks babes. You're the best," she says sweetly.

I feel sick with rage and leave immediately.

The following morning as the plane takes off I look out from my window seat and see the island disappear below me. The shimmering translucent shades of blue sea surrounding the island makes Malta appear to be an inviting paradise; but I now know better.

Twenty Three

As the plane makes its approach into London Gatwick, I'm reminded how beautiful England is from the air with the endless lush fields, like a patchwork quilt of pastel greens. I take my time as I consider whether to go through the red or green customs and excise channels. I decide that I have nothing I *want* to declare at the moment. Green it is then.

In my pocket is enough money for lunch and a taxi, but nothing more. I don't even have a driving licence anymore, so have little choice but to seek help, but from whom?

The options running through my mind are Jennifer, Stu, the Metropolitan Police Service, The Security Service or the National Crime Agency. I pass through customs and stand in contemplation just a couple of metres away from the front of the empty taxi rank, looking out into the London drizzle.

Given Jennifer may still be in a relationship with that lowlife Greg, I don't see how I can speak with her confidentially and it's unfair of me to expect Stu to help. As much as I want to see him, I can't justify the risk.

The problem with going to the authorities with accusations about Greg is that I have no evidence, and they're unlikely to believe me. Worse still, the authorities will run background checks on me and when they discover I faked my own death and have been using a forged passport, they will see to it that I'm locked away. This would be bad for me and also Stu, if Nicodemus loses patience. I need proof of Greg's crimes to convince the authorities to investigate, and since I don't have any evidence, then I'll have to seek help elsewhere.

I have very few friends and the majority of them would be of little help to me in my current predicament. I need someone who knew Greg, who I could trust. There's only one possibility, Ben from work. He had always seemed like a nice guy, but I hadn't socialised much with him before my 'death', other than going to a Halloween party at his house. Greg hadn't gone to that party and Ben's friends had seemed normal, so I figure Ben is the best person to go to. I'm due a lucky break.

There's now a small crowd of people queuing for taxis. Typical. I shuffle to the back of the line. I do eventually step out from under the shelter into the rain to claim my ride. I give the driver Ben's street name, but can't remember the house number.

My mind wanders during the drive through the London landscape. I hope that Nicodemus will keep his promise and that Dipa is now on her way home. I imagine how thrilled her family will be to see her again, after so long.

I think how Stu may react when he sees me again. I can't wait to see his smiling face. I feel smug in the knowledge that Greg is far from the poster boy he likes to portray himself as. I can't wait for the time when Jennifer discovers the truth about him.

I knew before my latest insight that Greg had little integrity, as he often exploited his contacts to get business and spread lies about the competition, but I had no idea that this extended to breaking the law and endangering lives. This darker side to Greg has been well hidden from his employees in the PI business.

"Where shall I drop you, Gov?" asks the London cabbie.

"Anywhere here is fine. Thanks."

I step out of the cab and notice the street is far longer than I remember. Thankfully the rain has stopped and the clouds disperse. It's almost three in the afternoon, so I've got some time before Ben returns from work. I walk the length of the street till I recognise the front of his house. I sit on the doorstep and wait.

"Hi Ben." I say as he walks towards me an hour later.

"What the *hell*! Joe. I thought you were dead?" Ben exclaims as he stops in his tracks.

"Yep. I was, but I'm back... Can I come in?"

"Umm. Yep, sure. Of course you can," Ben says. I step aside and he fumbles with his keys and opens the door. I follow him through to his kitchen where I lean against the counter, as he stares at me.

"Shit. What's going on Joe? It's good to see you," Ben says with his arms crossed.

"I need your help mate. I've been to hell and back and have nowhere else to go," I say. Ben looks on with concern.

"You're meant to be dead. I went to your *funeral*. Lots of people went. Your *wife cried*. There were flowers."

"I had to leave the country. I was being hunted by murderers. It was the only way to keep my family safe."

"What?" He said. "That doesn't make sense. Why the hell would you fake your own death?"

"I had to leave. It was the only way." I say.

I spend the next half hour recounting how Greg assigned me to find Dipa, which led me to a gang. I told Ben that this led me to a criminal in Malta who had told me that Greg was a major drug dealer.

"What about the police? Have you involved them?" Ben asks.

"No. Not yet. I need your help to get some evidence first."

"I guess, but what can I do?" Ben asks.

"I need to catch Greg's alter ego. Anything that proves his involvement in the movement/production of drugs. Can you help me?"

"Sure," Ben says unenthusiastically, "what's your plan?"

We spend the rest of that evening sitting at Ben's kitchen table brainstorming ideas of how to follow Greg. I figure that Alice holds Greg's diary so would likely know the next time that Greg disappears for one of his private meetings. These meetings were bound to provide him with an alibi while he got his hands dirty. We agree that Ben will get hold of Greg's diary from Alice and establish the date and location of his next visit. We had a plan.

I awake the next morning on Ben's settee as he creeps down the stairs in his suit. He grabs some breakfast while I lie still and stare at the ceiling.

"Want something to eat?" Ben shouts from next door.

"Not now. Thanks."

I hear the clang of a bowl and spoon as Ben eats. He walks in the room while he pulls his tie up and straightens it with the aid of the mirror on the wall in the corner of the room.

"So, you stay here today. Keep your head down. Don't contact anybody and I'll let you know what is going on tonight. Right?"

"Sounds good," I say, still snuggled under the blanket on the sofa, "see you later."

Ben unlocks a cabinet beneath the mirror and takes out something, before he closes the door and locks it again.

"Lunch money," he says, "keys." He taps is trouser pocket, "right, see you later."

Ben leaves and I spend the morning watching daytime television and eating breakfast. Ben's house is cramped and there's nothing to do. I get bored. I come across a digital voice recording device on the side, which gives me an idea. I check the microSD memory card inside the device, which is empty and ready to use. I start to chronicle my thoughts for the police, careful not to mention anything about Nicodemus.

Twenty Four

At midday I hear a fumble of keys at the front door. I break my stare from the television and look through the net curtains to see Greg and Ben together outside. What the hell is going on? Shit. I feel paralysed and time seems to stop ticking. I know that I can't escape as the backdoor is locked, plus Ben would easily catch me.

The adrenaline kicks in and I snap out of my trance and reach for the digital recording device. I press the record button. Whatever happens, I need to get this on tape. I place it carefully inside a drawer and stand in the middle of the room in nervous anticipation. I hear the front door open.

"Joe? It's Ben," he calls innocently.

I step into the hall and turn to see Ben with Greg. Greg stares at me with cold dispassionate eyes.

"What the hell!" I exclaim, hoping to persuade them that I was caught unawares.

Ben grabs my arms, walks me backwards into the living room and sits me on the settee. He stands over me with his arms crossed, like a bouncer on a daytime television chat show, and I'm some sort of unruly menace to society.

"Sorry Joe. There's been a change of plan."

I sit, unable and certainly unwilling to consider the consequences of what is happening. Greg takes his time. I hear the front door close and the clang of a coat hanger in the hallway, just beyond my sight. Greg eventually walks through the door, with a smile and wide open arms.

"Joe. What a surprise," he says, "don't get up on my account."

"What do you want?" I ask.

"Nothing. It's just so nice to see you alive. You're far more resourceful than I thought possible. Very clever, Joe. It does present us with a predicament though, what to do with you now?"

"You psychopath!" I yell, as Greg's mask of sanity shatters irreversibly.

"Very astute. My doctor says it's a misunderstood condition. I simply find myself to be more ambitious, confident and willing to push boundaries than the average man. But don't worry, I don't enjoy brutality. It's so primitive," Greg claims. "Ben, what shall we do with Joe?"

"Umm. I thought we were going to persuade him?" Ben says uncomfortably.

"Yes, of course. We can try that *first.*" Greg says.

"Ben, I thought we were friends," I say, as he looms above me.

"As you can tell, this meeting will end in one of two ways. One is certainly not preferred by any of us. So, let's talk about the alternative. As I see it, *you're* currently a fugitive of the state, not me."

"At least I'm only wanted for faking my own death. Unlike you drug dealers," I spit.

"Well actually, Joe, you're up to your neck in it. You see, how long have you worked for me?" Greg asks. "Five years or so, right?"

I nod.

"During that time you've been involved in your fair share of heinous crimes. Let me remind you of some. Well off the top of my psychopathic head, in August 2010 you found £40K that was stolen from me by a distributer. With your assistance, justice was swiftly served. More recently, just last year, you located an elderly couple who decided it was acceptable to take my product and run without payment. You helped me locate them so I could collect the unpaid debt. Shall I go on?"

"You know I didn't have any knowledge of what you were going to do with those people. I was just doing my job."

"The police don't know that," he says with a smile. "I don't want to hand you into the police though, or kill you. I'd prefer to work with you. You have talent and the best sort of anonymity. I mean if you're meant to be dead then just think what you can get away with."

"Who else knows about what you do? Does Jennifer?" I ask.

"Yep," he says, "she wants some adventure in her life. She found you so boring, but I get her excited. I fulfil her fantasies, Joe... Ben wanted me to get you involved long ago, but I knew you would never play nicely with us. It's ironic that you ended up becoming a wanted man, without any involvement from me."

"You forced me to run when you gave me that suicide mission," I say.

"You may have a point," Greg acknowledges with a smirk. "But when my associate's daughter was kidnapped suspiciously we had to investigate it ourselves."

"What?" I say.

"Has the penny dropped yet, Joe? Dipa's dad, Advik Sharma and his brother, Mukhtar, both work *with me*. We've built up the business together, and I *don't* mean the PI business. Whoever took Advik's daughter was sending a clear message to us. We thought we knew who it was, but had to be sure. Advik went public to keep the attention on Dipa, while Mukhtar, who has a low profile in this country, tasked you to do some digging around for us."

Wow. Ben strolls into the kitchen and I hear a tap turn on.

"You don't give me much choice, do you?" I say.

"That's the spirit. Now I want to know how this all unravelled. Ben told me a bit, but I want to know everything. I think I know what happened, but need to hear it from *you*," Greg says.

"It's just how I told Ben," I say, not wanting to reveal anything about Nicodemus.

Greg reaches into his pocket and takes out a lock knife. He opens the blade and presses it against my throat.

"I don't care much for Ben's upholstery. It's dated and needs changing," he says. "I'm going to tell you how I got my money back from that elderly couple."

"Okay," I mutter, as the steel blade stings my neck.

Ben walks through the door and drops his glass of water on the floor at the sight of a trickle of blood running down my neck.

"No, Greg, don't," Ben exclaims.

"Don't stain your pants. I'm telling Joe a story," Greg says cooly. "Well, as you should remember, you located those coffin dodgers in a little town outside of Brighton."

"Yes, I remember. They were in Heathfield. Mr. and Mrs. Peters, I think," I confirm as I hold still and grip my hands together to distract myself from the pain.

Ben gingerly picks up the larger shards of glass strewn on the floor, places them in a bowl and disappears back into the kitchen.

"They didn't have much money when I found them and had wasted most of my heroin. Since they couldn't pay me, then my compensation would be to kill them. I had always wondered what it felt like to kill. I mean, I've killed a cat when I was twelve, but that was with a gun and the thing deserved it for shitting in the garden. Anyway, I finally found out what it feels like to kill someone, well two people." Greg rants, "to be honest, I didn't much enjoy it. It's so messy. I spent the rest of the day cleaning up and disposing of their bodies in some lake nearby. I don't want to do the same thing again, but like I say, I'm sure Ben would benefit from a redecoration."

"Okay, I'll tell you the full story," I mutter. Greg takes the knife away and wipes the drops of blood from the blade onto Ben's sofa. "Right, so I tracked down this man who knew you. He knew all about your drug business. He had Dipa."

"Nicodemus," Greg said.

"Yes," I say, "how did you know?"

"I met him in 2011, after I tried to take advantage of a lead into the Maltese heroin market, which led to a dead-end. He threatened me, which hacked me off. I should've done something more direct instead of just pissing around with his business in the UK. What did he want from *you* then?"

"He wants me to expose you and your operation to the police. That's why I came to Ben. He said I would be safe if I did what he said. *That's* the truth," I say.

"Are we done here, now? It's been great to catch up with you Joe. I've got to get back to your wife now. Will you find it in your heart to forgive me?" he asks sarcastically.

"I'll work for you, again," I say, ignoring his last comment. "I don't have any other option. I can't go to the police, or back to Malta. What do you want me to do?" I ask.

"I need someone with your talents at the coalface of operations. As you appreciate, Ben and I don't have the time to oversee all the transactions and storage issues as well as holding down our day jobs. I currently rely on a real mixed bag of people. Not many of them have the proper motivation, unlike you. Do you think you can manage that?"

"Sure. Just tell me where and when," I say.

"Birmingham is the place. I have excellent police contacts who ensure we can do what we want at two warehouses just outside the city centre," he says and looks across at Ben, "Make sure he gets to Birmingham International Railway Station and hand him over to Tim. Keep your eyes on him. We don't want him changing his mind."

Ben nods.

"Don't screw it up, Joe. It's your last chance."

Twenty Five

Greg leaves in a hurry, which is a relief. He truly is a scary and powerful man. While Ben puts the broken glass outside in the rubbish bin, I stop the digital recorder and pocket the microSD memory card, before replacing the recorder where I first found it. Ben returns to the sitting room.

"Sorry about Greg. He gets very protective of his other company," Ben says.

Ben opens the locked cabinet under the mirror at the side of the room. Dozens of loose twenty pound notes flutter to the carpet. At the back of the cabinet there are wads of notes held together with elastic bands. There must be thousands and thousands stashed in there. He grabs a couple of hundred pounds and pushes the rest back in as he closes the door quickly.

"Now you're part of the club, Joe, there'll be plenty of this for you too," he says holding up a fistful of notes. "Let's get going now," Ben says and heads to the door.

We walk together to the train station and Ben buys two tickets. I take a free Metro newspaper at the station and we step onto the next train for London Waterloo. As the train pulls away, I read the cover story, about a former MP who had an affair with another MP's wife. No great surprise there, but great gossip. Page two reveals a picture of a smiling Indian girl. The accompanying article reads that '*a little girl called Dipa Sharma is to be reunited with her parents later today after being found against all odds by police in Malta, after wandering into the Anglican Cathedral in Valletta. The Maltese police described it as a miracle...*'

A shiver runs down my spine. I smile proudly and hit my knee with excitement. Dipa is free! Nicodemus was as good as his word.

"What's that all about, Joe?"

"Just a funny cartoon in the paper."

Ben stares at me as if I'm quite mad. I don't care. Then it hits me that Stu's life is now in real danger. Nicodemus will only wait so long before striking. I have to move fast to expose Greg, but can't while I'm being babysat.

As the train rolls into London Waterloo, the surroundings feel familiar but the circumstances are truly unique. Ben and I stroll through the barrier into Waterloo train station. Ahead I spot a Transport for London police officer heads down the steps to the toilets at the end of the station concourse.

Ben and I have a couple of minutes before our next train, so I wait until the policeman has disappeared from view, before I ask Ben if I can go to the toilet. I feel like a child at school. He glances across, sees no problems and nods his approval. He escorts me to the top of the steps, and thankfully allows me to go down by myself.

I enter the men's toilet area. The noise of hand driers blowing wet hands is quite overwhelming.

"Police. I need to talk to the policeman in here, now. It's urgent!" I yell loudly.

I reach into my pocket, take out the microSD card and stare at it. It contains the conversation about both Greg and Nicodemus; two of the biggest drug operators in Europe and a confession to a double murder. This thing is dynamite. Everything is becoming very real and frightening. I have to act fast before Ben looses patience and comes to find me.

The policeman exits a stall and while washing his hands, looks across to me.

"What's so urgent then?" he asks.

"I've got details of a double murder and two major drug dealers. I only have a minute before I have to go. Please write this down," I say.

"Do you now," he says sarcastically.

"My name's Joe Patterson from Crystal Palace. I've got information that must get to New Scotland Yard. I cannot talk now as I'm being watched. I've become involved in a drug cartel that provides heroin across the UK. This SD card has details of what is going on and also a confession of the double murder," I say as I present the micro chip.

He takes it and wipes his hands on his trousers before accepting it.

"Really?"

"Yes. I'm not a lunatic. My life is in danger. Please just give this to a detective in New Scotland Yard. My life does depend on it. I've got to go. Thanks."

"What's your date of birth, sir?" The officer calls as I walk towards the door.

"Technically, I'm deceased. The card has all the details," I say and open the door.

I hate being reliant on a police officer, but have no choice. He is now the gatekeeper to my freedom. I can do nothing more. I pray he takes me seriously and gets it to an detective quickly. That said, I'm not sure I would have taken my story seriously if someone had stopped me in the toilets.

I rush up the steps and meet Ben and we walk towards platform 12. We have three minutes till our train leaves.

We arrive at Birmingham just over two hours later and head to a pub just outside the station. It's late afternoon and the pub is getting crowded, with office workers and a few couples. Ben buys a couple of pints and we wait, sipping our drinks in silence, as I don't want to make small talk with someone who is effectively holding me hostage and clearly he can't wait to hand me over to his contact.

"Ben?" a young man asks with a Brummie twang and a teethy smile.

He's dressed in ripped jeans, a Metallica t-shirt and a badly fitted leather jacket, or maybe that's the style these days. I certainly wouldn't know.

"Hey Tim. How's it going?" Ben says. "This is him, Joe".

The grin evaporates from his acne scarred face as he sits opposite me. I notice a red mark across his forehead, like he has been wearing a tight hat.

"Alright, Joe," he grunts.

"Tim," I say. "What's the plan for this evening then?"

"Greg said to show ya round the place. He says you're here to stay. Where ya from?" Tim asks.

"That's not important," I mutter, not wanting to make friends. "Let's go then."

I scrape back my bar stool from the table and stand. I leave Ben still nursing the remainder of his drink, as I can't be with him for a moment longer. I prefer to be anywhere else, even if it means putting up with Tim, my new adolescent minder.

"Keep a close eye on him, Tim," Ben warns as I walk away from the table.

Tim follows and we leave the bright lights of the pub and enter the evening gloom.

"Are we driving?" I ask.

"Yeah, my ride's just down 'ere," Tim says.

We walk down a side street. Greg must have been desperate for staff if he has Tim on the books. The boy is barely seventeen. He presses the unlock button on his keys and a yellow Mercedes S-Class lights up, parked partly on the pavement.

"Subtle."

"It's a wicked car," Tim says.

As we drive away, Tim turns on some rap music, which blares from the surround sound speaker system. I instinctively turn it off. Tim barely reacts. After a ten minute drive we arrive at some gated warehouses on a trading estate, which are surrounded by a six foot fence with anti-climb paint. There are no windows on either building, just large front facing bay doors, which are closed, and two side doors. There's no sign of life. Tim leaves the engine running and steps out to remove the padlocks from the front gate. We drive onto the tarmac between two warehouses.

"This is your new palace," Tim says. "You'll love it."

I step out of the car, and not for the first time feel like a criminal, arriving at a drug den in a pimped car, at night in a dodgy neighbourhood. Tim locks the gate and we stroll together to the side door of one of the warehouses. What the hell am I doing here? I feel nervous but don't let it show.

Tim unlocks the door and reaches inside, his fingers find a large industrial light switch. Click. Rows and rows of lights flicker on in unison. I step into the warehouse to witness the scale of Greg's business. It's overwhelming. There are hundreds, maybe thousands of cardboard boxes stacked five high in the giant warehouse, which must be close to a hundred metres in length.

"You live in *here*?"

"Yeah, at the back," Tim says, pointing to a bed, way in the back corner.

"Wow," I chuckle nervously, "it's quite a place."

I step forward and take a closer look at a forklift truck, but Tim grabs my arm.

"You need to wear overalls before going any further."

It's only then that I notice the mat on the floor where we are standing. It's a six foot square blue mat with three plastic chairs along one edge, strewn with white overalls. Next to the chairs there are two boxes labelled 'Gloves' and 'Hair Nets'.

"What's this all about?" I ask.

"We can't leave any trace when handlin' stuff. No finger prints or hairs. Everythin' has to be neat and done proper," Tim says confidently, coming into his own.

I look around again, the warehouse was immaculately organised. The boxes were placed in tidy rows and size ordered. Everything clearly had its place, probably thanks to Tim. I finally appreciate why Greg got this guy. Tim's a neat freak, which I imagine is just what you need in any warehouse business.

"Do I get the grand tour?" I ask, as we each pull on our extra layers of clothing.

I feel like a forensic scientist whose entering a crime scene, from a movie. Actually, thinking about it, I am in a crime scene. Frightening thought.

"The outfit is a bit tight. Do you wear it all the time?"

"Yep, everywhere in the warehouse, apart from on my mat at the back, where my bed and bathroom is and the mat we're on now," Tim explains.

"That's dedication. I don't think I can do this all the time."

"You will," Tim insists.

On that sober thought, Tim takes me round. We start at the front, passing the forklift truck, which has oil stains running down the back of it and a torn leather seat. It looks like a fun drive though.

"We get two types of delivery, heroin and products. We 'ave to get the drugs into the stuff and send them on their way. Over 'ere are the boxes of drugs," he says, pointing to the left of the warehouse at a hundred or so boxes.

"*All* those boxes contain heroin?" I ask.

"Yeah. It's busy right now."

"Okay," I say, in a daze.

"In the middle are the things to hide the drugs in. We've got microwaves, toasters and vases at the moment. Over there's where the finished boxes are kept, until they're collected."

"I'm impressed. What's in the other warehouse then?" I ask.

A mobile rings from the other side of the warehouse. Tim turns and runs back to the mat at the far side to answer the call. I stay where I am.

"Yep. Hi," I hear Tim say from a distance, before he lowers his tone to a whisper. He puts his mobile back on the chair.

"Everything okay?" I yell.

"Yep," Tim shouts back quickly, as he goes to the side door, where we had entered.

I hear a jangle of keys and a clicking sound. He's locked the door. Why? He walks briskly to his communal area at the back, out of sight. Everything makes me jumpy at the moment. I need to chill out and stop winding myself up for no good reason. He returns with what looks like a sleeping bag.

"Let's set you up for the night. You can sleep here," he says pointing at the other blue mat, further away from the door.

"Not exactly the Hilton, is it?" I say, trying to break the tension.

"Nope," Tim says dryly and walks away.

I maybe more paranoid than usual, but Tim's attitude to me seems to have changed since the phone call. I step inside the unrolled sleeping bag. I settle down for the night on my unusual mattress, as I use some screwed up overalls as a pillow.

There's another jangle of keys and the door opens again. I tilt my head from the laying position, to see Tim looking back at me as he steps outside. His hand flicks the lights off, so I suddenly feel like I'm inside a long tunnel, with a single light from outside shining through the distant door into the darkness. He slams the door and the noise echoes between the corrugated metal walls of my new prison. I wriggle down inside my sleeping bag and stare into the inky blackness.

Twenty Six

I wake and it's still pitch black. I remind myself that it maybe daylight outside, but I'd never know it. I remain calm and lie where I am, waiting. What seems like twenty minutes later I hear a distant scratching sound and then the warehouse side door opens, providing a narrow channel of sunlight to stretch out across the vast empty space.

I sit up in my sleeping bag and look down the width of the building, to see Tim step into the building and clicks the light on, which lights up the cavernous warehouse with the yellowish light from the rack of lamps way above my head.

I get up, stretch and roll up the sleeping bag, as Tim closes and locks the door again. It is bitterly cold in here. I can see my breath rising in the air. I put on a set of overalls to warm myself. Tim walks down.

"Mornin'. Help yourself to the toilet at the back," he yells as he puts on some overalls.

I walk towards the back and find a square plastic portable toilet. I open the flimsy door and climb into the box. A spring slams it shut behind me as I empty my bladder into the pool of blue liquid beneath. I wash my hands, throw water onto my face and look at my still brown complexion in the mirror. There is no chance of maintaining my tan if I'm going to be stuck in here for eternity.

"What the hell are you doing here, Joe?" I ask the mirror.

I don't have a toothbrush and wonder how I can buy supplies around here. I hope I'm free to leave when I want. I open the door and see lots of people who have appeared from nowhere. I nearly have a heart attack, step back and the door slams shut again. I peek out of the door again to see maybe fifty people all wearing suits and hairnets crawling all over the warehouse. I step out carefully. Were they police officers?

"Joe. Come over here," Tim shouts and waves at me at the same time, as he too looks like one of the many uniformed clones now wondering around.

I step out of the plastic bathroom and walk towards Tim. They must be workers. Tim is in charge and directs the workers. They must sleep and live in the warehouse next door. It all makes sense. Tim can't possibly run the whole place by himself.

The army of men and women work together like bees in a hive. Some are moving boxes, while others unscrew the back of a microwave, add polystyrene pieces into vases and one man operates the forklift, stacking all the finished boxes at the far end. It's a symphony of covert drug packaging.

There's one particularly tall well built guy who stood next to Tim, also wearing the standard warehouse fashion.

"Joe. This is Paul," Tim says as I approach. "Paul's in charge of security. I want you to stay with him till Ben arrives. Okay?"

"Hi Paul," I say as his massive hand envelopes mine completely and squeezes it tight. Paul has a tattoo of a crucifix on the left of his neck and a nose ring, which, with his wide eyes, makes him look like a raging bull.

"Let's go play some pool," Paul says.

"Why not," I say, not willing to disagree with the big guy.

My new friend, Paul, and I head out of the opposite side door and cross a narrow alley. We enter the adjacent warehouse, which appears to be of the same dimensions. I notice Paul, the man mountain, has to duck to get into the place to avoid hitting his head.

There's clearly no need for overalls in here, as it's set up to cater for people rather than class A drugs. There are bunk beds along one side, in between row upon row of wardrobes. Next there are three kitchen areas complete with lino flooring, a cinema area with lines of chairs and several pool tables.

A cluster of toilets and showers run down the length of the middle of the space and on the far side there are about forty cars of all makes and colours. I guess they must be owned by the workers.

It's all very sterile. The concrete floor and harsh overhead lighting dominate the feel of the place. Clearly they've tried to dress it up as best they can, to make it more homely, but it's still a cold and dark warehouse. It had all the appeal of prison living quarters, in fact at least in a prison you get assigned your own room and have proper central heating. It must get freezing in here during the winter months.

During our pool game, I quickly notice that although Paul is not much of a speaker, he's very talented with a cue. He sinks ball after ball with no error. He clearly spends a lot of his time on the table. We're interrupted by Ben's arrival. He looks annoyed. I put my pool cue down on the table.

"Hi Joe. Me again," Ben says from a distance without a smile and approaching fast.

"Hello Ben. You just saved me from being beaten six nil. Paul is a great player," I say, trying to break the ice.

"I've driven a long way. I'm not interested in small talk," Ben says stopping just short of my toes and stares me down. I feel his breath on my face.

"Sure," I mutter nervously.

"Did you use my recorder?" he barks.

"What?" I ask, as my heart sinks into my stomach.

"Greg was very clear about your options yesterday. You screwed it right up, so I'm here to *kill* you," Ben says, as he takes his jacket off.

"I did use it, yes. Sorry. I wanted to capture some of my thoughts. Umm. I used it. Yes," I gabble while Paul grabs my arms and holds them behind me. I get the feeling he's used to handling people in this way.

Ben thumps me in the face and I hear a crack and an explosion of pain from my nose. I see double for a second and lean over to see blood drip to the floor.

"Where's the bloody memory stick, Joe?" Ben asks slowly. "Once again you have two options. You can die quickly or slowly. Which do you want?" he pulls me up and slaps me gently on the cheeks, in an effort to get my attention.

My heads spins and I cough as I choke on my own blood as it trickles down the back of my throat.

"I thought we were friends?" I spit.

"I'm not your friend. You're a bad judge of character. You've been played the whole time," Ben says and throws in a punch to my kidneys for good measure.

"I threw it away. I want to work here. I need the money. Please..." I plead.

"Where?" he asks, as he raises his clenched fist above his head.

Paul holds my arms like a vice and I tense in anticipation of the pain. Thankfully Ben never hits me, as he's distracted by distant screams. People come sprinting through the side door from the adjacent warehouse, still wearing their white overalls.

"Police!" someone yells.

"Impossible," Ben mutters and turns to me. "What the hell have you done?"

More people run through the door. Through my watering eyes I make out one person running to the front of the warehouse and press a large blue button. The huge bay doors begin to creak and the shutter door slowly rolls open, letting the sunlight into the gloom. Paul dumps me like a sack of coal and lumbers, as best as a heavyweight can, towards the cars at the side of the room.

"Who's the bad judge of character now?" I yell, as I hold my nose. "You'd better run, Ben."

Ben runs after Paul as I collapse to my knees. The pain across my face pulsates. Twenty or so other people sprint by me, as I lie on the floor, with the beautiful sunshine bathing my squinting eyes.

I hear the roar of engines as they start along the edge of the warehouse. I tilt my head to see cars swerve out from the queue and the tyres squeal as it accelerates towards the still expanding gap at the front of the warehouse. Another car drives straight through three toilets and a wash cubicle in the driver's haste for freedom. Two of the portable loos tumble over on the side and blue water gushes out of the open door and runs across the concrete. Tyre smoke, petrol fumes and dust fill the air. I cough. Blood splatters from my mouth.

I see police officers in riot gear jump onto everyone wearing overalls and pulling their arms behind them. The police use plastic cable ties to hold their wrists and ankles together and then move to the next person.

I remain there on the dusty floor, exhausted, holding my bleeding and broken nose. Police officers bellow warnings that fill the air. The electric door opens wide enough for me to have a clear view of four police cars blocking the front gate. Some people climb over the barbed wire topped fence line, only to be wrestled by police on the other side.

Paul tries unsuccessfully to ram a police riot van with his jeep, only to vent black smoke from his car. He's tasered when he leaves his vehicle. Four officers are quickly on top of him, to prevent any chance of escape for the big man. I lose track of Ben but am quite certain he must be caught also.

Eventually an officer walks over to me and helps me to my feet, before cuffing my hands and leading me away with the others. A man wearing jeans and a shirt intercepts my path to the back of a police car.

"Joe?" the plain clothes officer asks me as he flashes a police warrant card.

"That's me. Joe Patterson," I say, never happier to admit my true name.

The two officers exchange whispered words before the policeman who's escorting me releases my hands from the handcuffs.

"I'm Detective Inspector Vangelis Fraser, from New Scotland Yard. Please come with me. I want to get you out of here quickly," The plain clothed officer says.

"Thank you, Detective Inspector. Did you get my recording?"

"I certainly did."

"Can I ask that you collect my son, Stuart, please?"

"He's already in protective custody."

Twenty Seven

We stop at a Birmingham hospital, where a doctor confirms my nose is broken and that only the passing of time will heal it. Apparently, I'm destined to look like a boxer. They give me pain killers, which numbs my throbbing nose.

Afterwards, Detective Inspector Vangelis puts the police lights on his unmarked police car and drives us along the M6 and into London, sometimes making use of the hard shoulder to avoid the heavy traffic. Several speed cameras go off as he gets up to 130mph, whizzing past cars, vans, motorbikes. Vangelis seems calm and coordinated, while I grip the pull down handle on the ceiling so tightly that I lose feeling in my hand.

He takes us to New Scotland Yard, the headquarters of the London Metropolitan Police Service. As we drive past the front entrance, I recognise the distinctive slowly rotating triangular sign from the news. I keep my head down as there are a handful of paparazzi snapping at the car and every other car near the building.

"What's with all the cameras?" I ask Vangelis as we turn into the underground garage at the side of the imposing police building.

"The drug raid this morning made the headlines," Vangelis says. "There'll be a lot of interest in this case when the media get the full story."

He parks under the building and we head up in a lift. Once again I find myself walking into a small interview room, but this time I can be certain that this *is* a police station. It's only at this point in time that I have the opportunity to see that Vangelis is a short, slight man, with Oriental ancestry, a wide nose and dark hair. He has kind brown eyes.

"Can I get you a tea, coffee, orange juice?" Vangelis asks.

"An orange juice would be great. Thanks. Is there any chance of getting something to eat too?"

"I tell you what. Let's get out of here and go to the restaurant. The food's not great, but it's better than being trapped in here."

"Thanks," I say.

We head to the top floor by lift and walk into the staff restaurant. I take a seat by the window while Vangelis buys me a sandwich and orange juice from the staff sandwich bar. The view of Big Ben, Green Park and the Thames is fantastic. I touch my nose. I feel self conscious with cotton wool stuffed up each nostril.

"How are you feeling?"

"Tired. I'm tired of running. I can't do it anymore."

"You don't have to," Vangelis says and pulls out a small evidence bag from his shirt pocket containing the microSD memory card. "This means you can stop running. It's gold dust. The implications of this recording go far beyond Greg Webber and his drug network. There's the international angle and the matter of police corruption too. No one yet knows how high up the betrayal goes. That was the main reason for our delay in rescuing you. We simply didn't know who to trust in the West Midlands Constabulary. After a surveillance team followed you to the warehouse yesterday evening, we worked all night to coordinate a response from London, bypassing the usual local involvement. Let me tell you, that generated a lot of red tape."

"What about my wife, Jennifer?"

"She's been arrested, on suspicion of being an accomplice."

"My god," is all I could manage.

"It's a shock, I'm sure. Our investigations have just started, but it looks like she has known about Greg's business for several months."

"What about Dipa?"

"A consular assistant from the British High Commission has collected her. She will be home tomorrow morning-"

"That's fantastic! I'm so," I pause as I watch Vangelis' face drop.

"Err, unfortunately, Dipa's parents have also been arrested."

"...What happens now then?" I ask.

"Well I would strongly suggest that you enter witness protection, with your son. There could be a lot of people who want to come after you."

"Not me, no way. I will *not* be reliant on the police for help... You see Vangelis... my brother was killed two years ago by a police officer driving recklessly," I say holding back the tears. "Ever since then I have preferred never to be reliant on the police for anything," I say heatedly.

A couple of police officers on the next table shuffle in their chairs and glance at us. I instantly feel bad for taking out my frustrations out on Vangelis. It doesn't help that I feel completely deflated by the news of Jennifer and Dipa's parents.

"I'm sorry. I know you're just trying to help me," I say.

"I can't guarantee your safety without your cooperation," Vangelis whispers.

"Have you made any other copies of this?" I ask as I pick up the memory chip in the evidence bag.

Vangelis shakes his head.

"This is my son's death sentence. Nicodemus is a powerful man. I can't let his name become involved in this investigation," I say waving the memory chip at Vangelis. "I can't let you have it."

I must destroy it. I pull my chair back from the coffee table and run towards the door of the restaurant kitchen. Police officers in the restaurant do nothing more than stare as I run by. Vangelis follows in haste but shouts nothing; I can only guess this is because of the embarrassment factor. I just stole an exhibit from his hands while inside his headquarters.

I swing open the kitchen door and look around in desperation. The flames from the grill wouldn't work. A kitchen knife would only cause superficial damage, a deep fat fryer may work, but then I notice a sign above the kitchen sink, '*Keep hands away when operating the Waste Disposal Unit*'. Perfect.

"Hey, what are you doing in here?" a chef calls.

I run to the sink, tear open the evidence bag and pull out the memory card. I turn the sink tap on and force the chip into the waste unit and press the start button on the wall. There is a horrible noise of tortured metal and a rattle that quickly turns into a continuous metallic tinkling sound. I keep the unit going till a chef pulls me away from the button. I'm confident the memory card is completely destroyed, beyond any hope of recovery.

"What the hell did you do that for?" Vangelis asks furiously. "You're under arrest for the destruction of police evidence."

I hold my hands in front of me. I have nowhere to run and I don't want to run anyway. Vangelis cuffs me.

"I don't understand why you destroyed the memory card. That proved you're innocent of any crimes."

"Like I said, there's more on that recording than I can allow you to use in court," I say.

"What's so special about this Nicodemus guy then?" he asks, as he leads me back to the open lift door.

"I'm sorry officer. I have *no* recollection of any Nicodemus," I say sarcastically, as the door shuts and we go down into the bowels of the building.

"Okay. You can speak off the record. I just want to know what this is all about," he says, as we reach the interview room.

"No. It's better this way. No one can protect me from him. He's got powerful links across Europe. I'm better just withholding anything about him. I'm not going to give evidence."

We sit in the interview room and Vangelis presses start on the installed tape recorder on the table.

"Joe Patterson. I have some evidence that implicates your links to Malta," Vangelis says slyly. "The note you gave to the taxi driver before your apparent demise."

"I remember that it gives the address of the Shere farmhouse, where I discovered the body," I say.

"It also gave us something else, Joe. You see our forensics lab found another address on it," he explains.

"How?" I ask, confused.

"It was an imprint on the paper. The paper was from a notebook, correct?" he asks.

"Yes, this one," I say and pull out my little black notebook.

"Well you wrote another address on a piece of paper above the one you gave to the taxi driver. The imprint of the other note was on the paper. The point is that we have evidence that links you to a specific address in Malta," he says.

"Please stop the recorder," I beg.

Vangelis slowly places a finger on the stop button and pushes. The reels stop turning.

"Please destroy that exhibit," I plead.

"No, I can't do that. What I could do though is... overlook it when we go to court. There'll be a lot of evidence and it may get lost. I can only do this if you cooperate fully with me. I want everything you have on Greg Webber, his associates and any bent policemen you know."

"Okay, but nothing on Nicodemus, okay? Do I get full immunity from prosecution if I do what you want?" I ask.

"Probably. We'll have to see," Vangelis says, with a grin.

He presses the button on the voice recorder once again. The tape turns.

"Let's continue, Joe Patterson," Vangelis says.

Epilogue

It seems to have taken forever for today to arrive. My normal routine has been turned upside down since my return to England. I've had to keep a low profile, because of press interest. I hope that after today my current state of limbo will disappear and I can start to rebuild my life.

I sit in the back of an unmarked police car at eight in the morning. It's a frosty and misty morning, as we meander the streets of London. Despite being treated like a VIP by my police escorts and bought coffee, I'm still in a daze and not in the mood to talk with anyone, especially not the equally solemn officer in casual dress sat alongside me at the time. I glance out of the side window and see the bronze Lady Justice hanging above the rooftops, getting closer as we park up at the side door of the Old Bailey Central Criminal Court.

I hesitate as there appears to be a media scrum on the other side of my door, between me at the courthouse. I'm dressed to impress, in a new suit and about to walk through the entrance they are monitoring, which will undoubtedly draw their attention.

I swallow any doubt I've got about my safety and leave the car with the minimal of fuss, stepping onto the pavement while my escort strides around the back of the vehicle, to assist me.

"Are you giving evidence today?" yells one journalist while he pushes a microphone into my face. The journalist's arm is quickly wrestled aside by my new best friend, as I force my way through the melee of hungry paparazzi. "Are you afraid for your life?" came the follow on question, despite my unresponsiveness.

A couple of flashes dazzle my eyes. I keep my head down and walk briskly towards the door. "What's it like to be responsible for the resignation of the Home Secretary?" yells another.

The press have been dining out on one of the biggest police scandals in history. *'Class A-Gate'*, as the press have nicknamed it, highlighted corruption in the police ranks that went all the way to the top. Money seems to have been accepted by senior police officials in exchange for looking the other way, while vast quantities of drugs were imported and distributed across the UK.

Other government departments also felt the heat, especially the National Crime Agency and Home Office. Inevitably, as further details of this repugnant affair surfaced, there has been genuine public anger. Heads had to roll. The scalp of the Home Secretary seems to have quenched the immediate public bloodlust.

I reach the large front doors and enter the grand and old fashioned building. I'm quickly processed through the metal detector, manned by a overzealous young man, and meet Vangelis, who's also dressed smartly in a suit and tie.

"Today is *your* day, Joe," Vangelis says, as he hugs me. "You feeling okay?"

For the past couple of weeks, he has been encouraging me, like a football manager who has signed a young and very talented striker. He wanted me to perform well on the day. I suppose his career will benefit if do well in the witness box today.

"Nervous as hell, but otherwise fine," I say.

"You'll be great. Just relax."

The two of us walk in sync through a couple of corridors and up several staircases, till we reach court 413. Inside there are lawyers everywhere, with their briefcases, talking in whispers and shaking hands with each other warmly. The whole thing stinks of the old boys' network in action. I feel completely out of place. I look up to the public gallery and see Stu and a minder in the front row. Stu smiles widely and waves enthusiastically.

I've become a fulltime single parent since Jennifer was arrested. I've accepted that my relationship with her is fractured beyond all repair, after all, it is my evidence that has put her behind bars.

Since my return, Jennifer and I have only spoken twice, by telephone, in the briefest of exchanges. On the second occasion we agreed custody rights for Stu. We were both keen to talk directly about this matter, rather than through a lawyer, as it saved a lot of money on something we both agreed; a 50:50 split of his time, after she is released, which her lawyer assesses will be in six months time. Only time will show how bitter the divorce will become.

Vangelis leads us to our usual seats, where we can survey the drama. Over the last few days I've attended to get used to the format and questioning style. It's been like watching a Shakespearean play. There is the pompous judge with his wig and the lawyers all speaking old fashioned English, with strange and wonderful legal terms. The claims and counter claims are all delicately poised, like a game of chess. It all terrifies me.

After a few minutes of boisterous chatter, a court official steps up to the judge's chair and announces "All rise for Judge John Malcolm Wilkinson QC."

We all get to our feet and fall silent, in a show of respect. The judge, an old man wearing a long robe, the obligatory wig and a permanent stern look on his face, sits quickly. He shuffles some papers and reaches for a large lever-arch file.

"This is day nineteen of the case of the Crown Prosecution Service versus the Birmingham twenty three. Let us open with a statement from the prosecution," the judge says quickly and without looking any further around the court than his own notes.

Vangelis had told me previously that the twenty three people standing trial include both of the Sharma brothers, some of the warehouse staff, including Tim, and a few employees from 'Professional & Confidential Investigations Bureau Ltd', notably Ben. I was pleased to learn that Alice had been as naive to the whole affair as I had been.

The prosecution barrister, stands. He's a tall man with deep furrows in his forehead, no doubt brought on by years of intense learning and verbal jousting in courtrooms like this one. He's only a few seats away from me and wears a black gown. He leans against his lectern, briefly studies a piece of paper before him and then addresses the court.

"Thank you, Your Honour," he says. "I'll start by saying that it appears the defendants have been particularly devious in their attempts to conceal the extent of the smuggling operation that has clearly been running for many months, if not far longer. The Metropolitan Police Service has evidence that indicates that the origins of the network may have begun as long ago as 2007. Of course, due to the unfortunate position we find ourselves in today of not being able to question Mr. Gregory John Webber, we may never know the full details."

"It has been noted. Go on," the judge says grandly.

"It should also be noted that the Metropolitan Police Service continues to liaise with Interpol on the whereabouts of Mr. Webber. Mr. Webber was last seen boarding a plane from Gatwick Airport on 4 September 2012, destined for Malta. However the Maltese authorities have had difficulty confirming whether Mr. Webber ever arrived in their country," the barrister pauses at this point and looks up at the judge briefly, maybe for dramatic effect. "Of course the police investigation continues and if any new developments occur during the hearing, then we will, of course, make these available to the court, Your Honour, as quickly as possible."

"I am most grateful for your efforts," the judge says with a smile.

"And so, today I would like to call Witness B to the stand, if you are content Your Honour?" the prosecuting barrister asks.

I feel a lump in my throat. I am Witness B. My hands go all sweaty. It's finally my time. This was part of the deal I agreed with Vangelis months before to protect my identity.

"Your witness may proceed," the judge instructs.

I make my way to the witness box at the front and stand in front of my seat ready to be sworn in, facing back into the court. I look up and see Stu smiling in the crowd.

27641080R00125

Printed in Great Britain
by Amazon